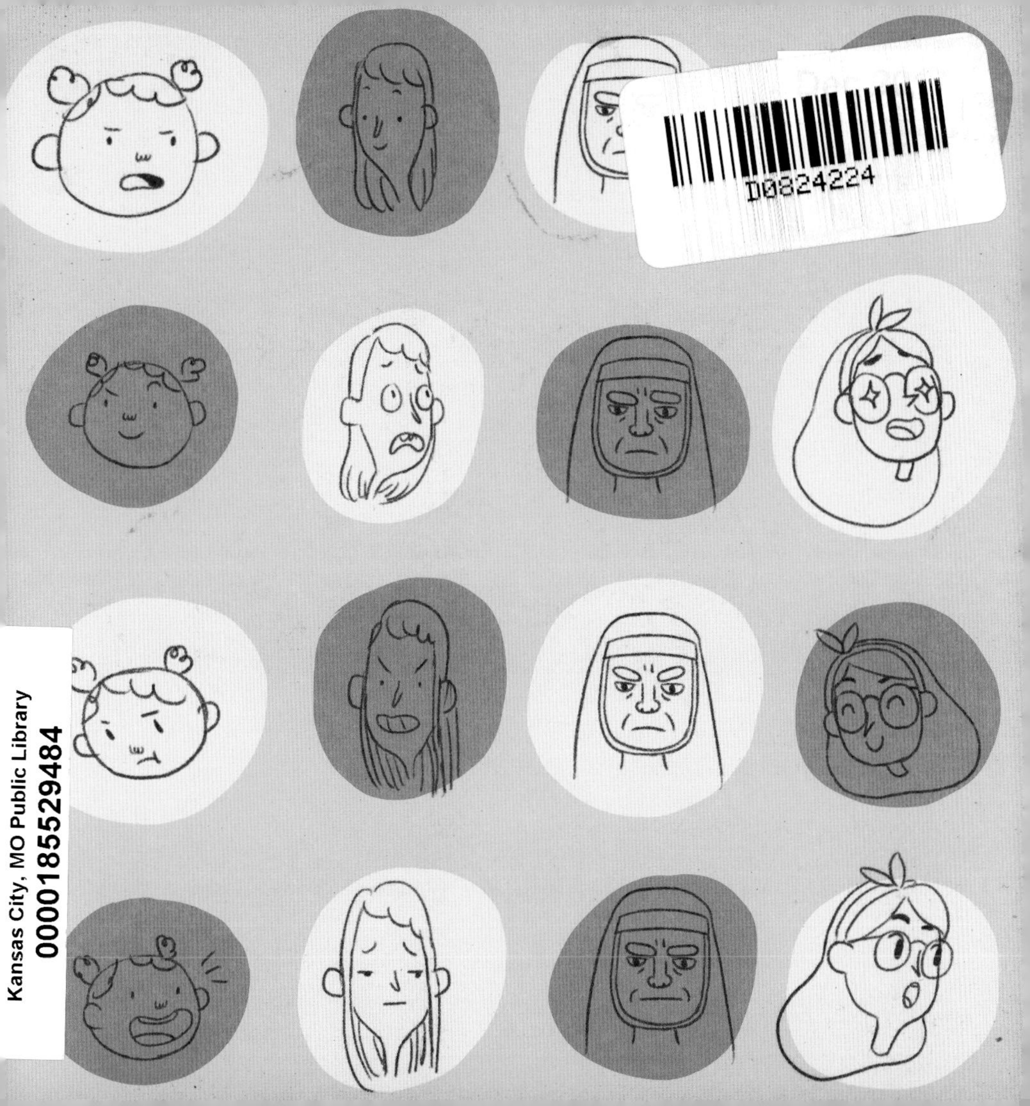

The Short Con
Pops & Branwell Mysteries Vol. 1
by Pete Toms and Aleks Sennwald

Published by Study Group Comics
www.studygroupcomics.com

Printed in China by New Titan Print.

ISBN 978-1-68148-008-4

the
SHORT CON

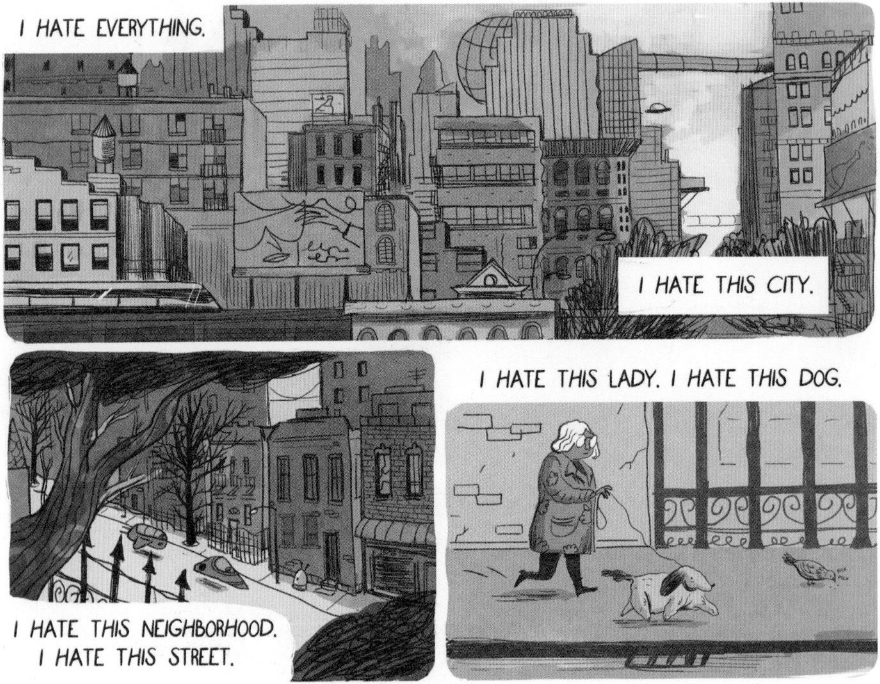
I HATE EVERYTHING.
I HATE THIS CITY.
I HATE THIS NEIGHBORHOOD.
I HATE THIS STREET.
I HATE THIS LADY. I HATE THIS DOG.

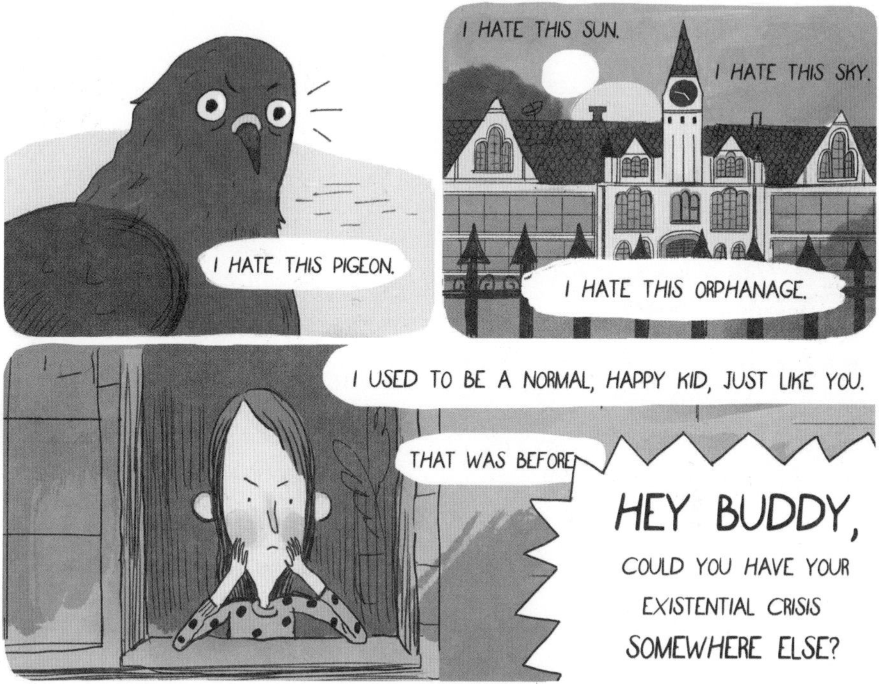
I HATE THIS PIGEON.
I HATE THIS SUN.
I HATE THIS SKY.
I HATE THIS ORPHANAGE.
I USED TO BE A NORMAL, HAPPY KID, JUST LIKE YOU.
THAT WAS BEFORE
HEY BUDDY,
COULD YOU HAVE YOUR EXISTENTIAL CRISIS SOMEWHERE ELSE?

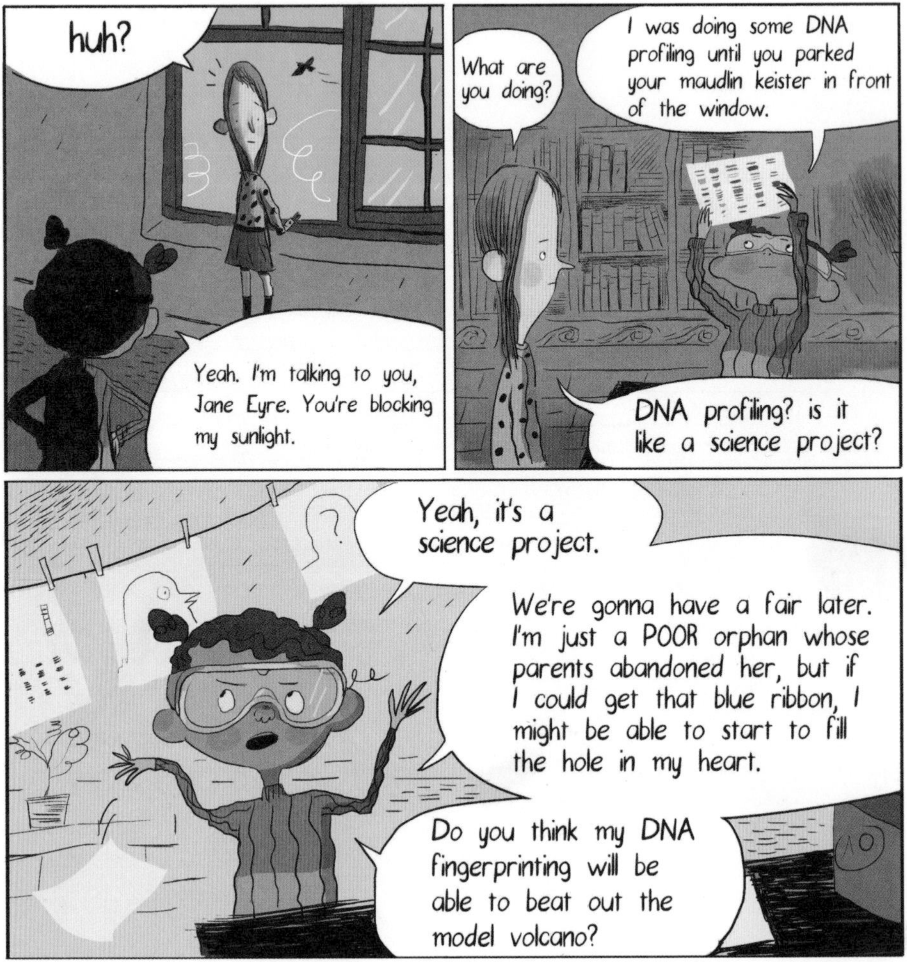
huh?
Yeah. I'm talking to you, Jane Eyre. You're blocking my sunlight.
What are you doing?
I was doing some DNA profiling until you parked your maudlin keister in front of the window.
DNA profiling? is it like a science project?
Yeah, it's a science project.
We're gonna have a fair later. I'm just a POOR orphan whose parents abandoned her, but if I could get that blue ribbon, I might be able to start to fill the hole in my heart.
Do you think my DNA fingerprinting will be able to beat out the model volcano?

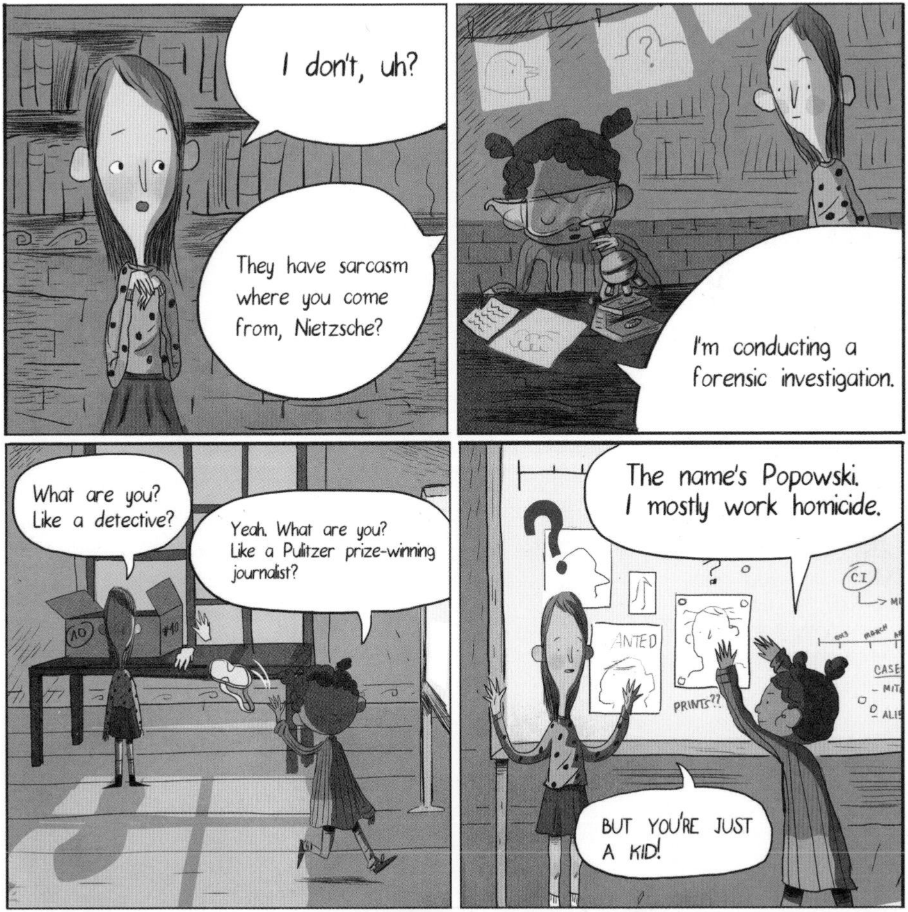
I don't, uh?
They have sarcasm where you come from, Nietzsche?
I'm conducting a forensic investigation.
What are you? Like a detective?
Yeah. What are you? Like a Pulitzer prize-winning journalist?
The name's Popowski. I mostly work homicide.
BUT YOU'RE JUST A KID!

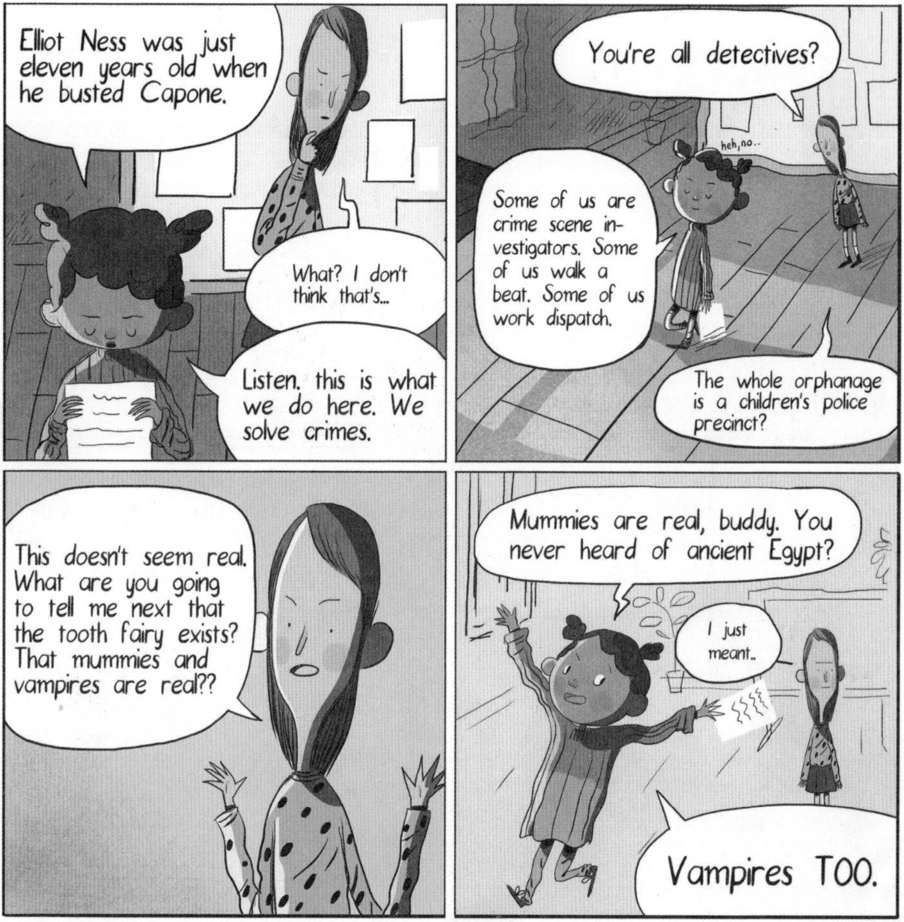
Elliot Ness was just eleven years old when he busted Capone.
What? I don't think that's...
Listen, this is what we do here. We solve crimes.
You're all detectives?
heh, no..
Some of us are crime scene investigators. Some of us walk a beat. Some of us work dispatch.
The whole orphanage is a children's police precinct?
This doesn't seem real. What are you going to tell me next that the tooth fairy exists? That mummies and vampires are real??
Mummies are real, buddy. You never heard of ancient Egypt?
I just meant..
Vampires TOO.

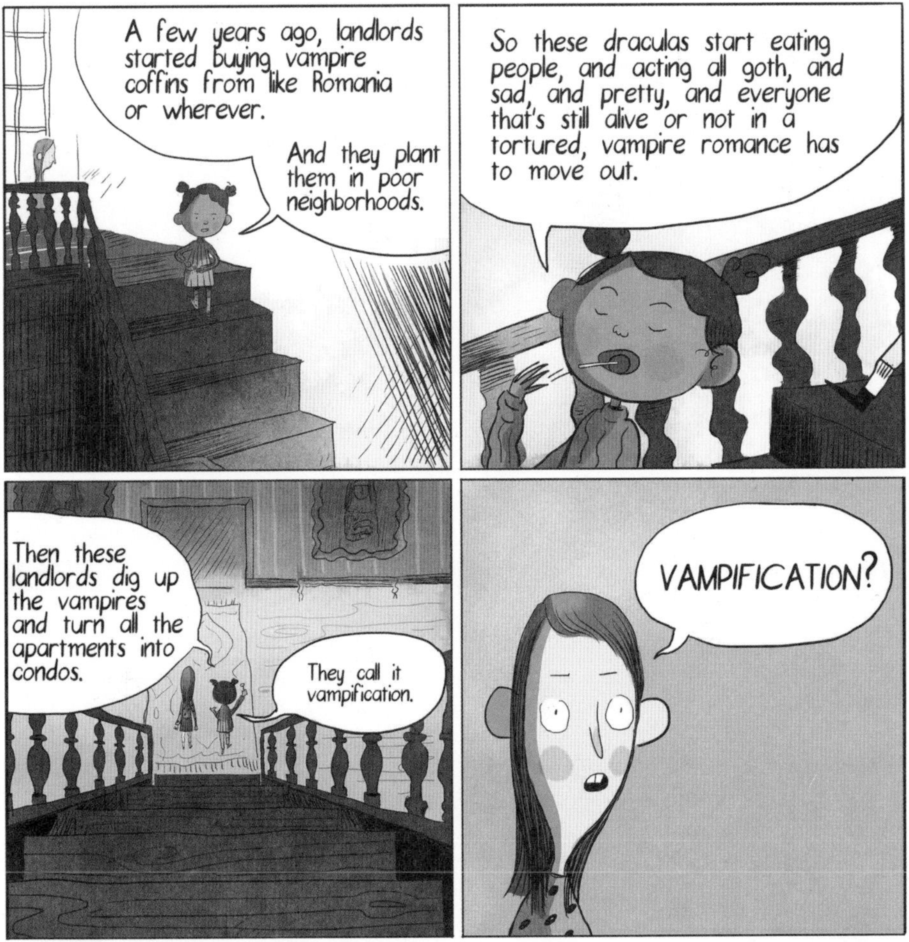
A few years ago, landlords started buying vampire coffins from like Romania or wherever.
And they plant them in poor neighborhoods.
So these draculas start eating people, and acting all goth, and sad, and pretty, and everyone that's still alive or not in a tortured, vampire romance has to move out.
Then these landlords dig up the vampires and turn all the apartments into condos.
They call it vampification.
VAMPIFICATION?

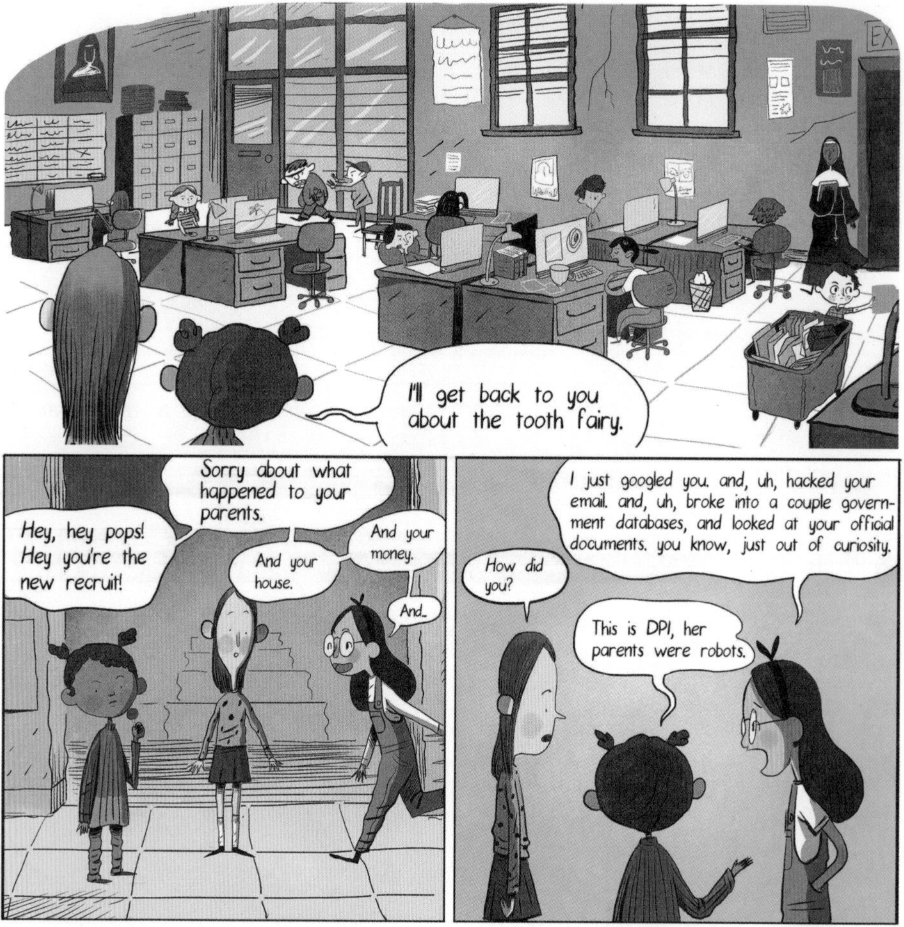
I'll get back to you about the tooth fairy.
Hey, hey pops! Hey you're the new recruit!
Sorry about what happened to your parents.
And your house.
And your money.
And...
How did you?
I just googled you. and, uh, hacked your email. and, uh, broke into a couple government databases, and looked at your official documents. you know, just out of curiosity.
This is DPI, her parents were robots.

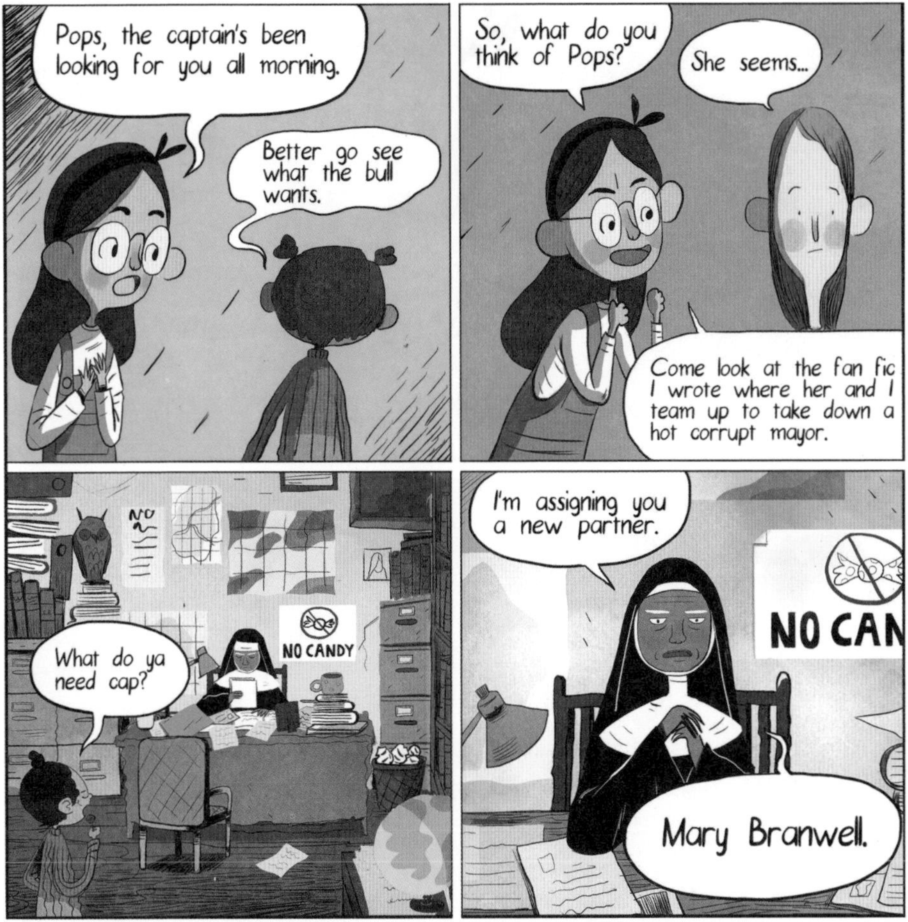
Pops, the captain's been looking for you all morning.
Better go see what the bull wants.
So, what do you think of Pops?
She seems...
Come look at the fan fic I wrote where her and I team up to take down a hot corrupt mayor.
NO CANDY
What do ya need cap?
I'm assigning you a new partner.
NO CAN
Mary Branwell.

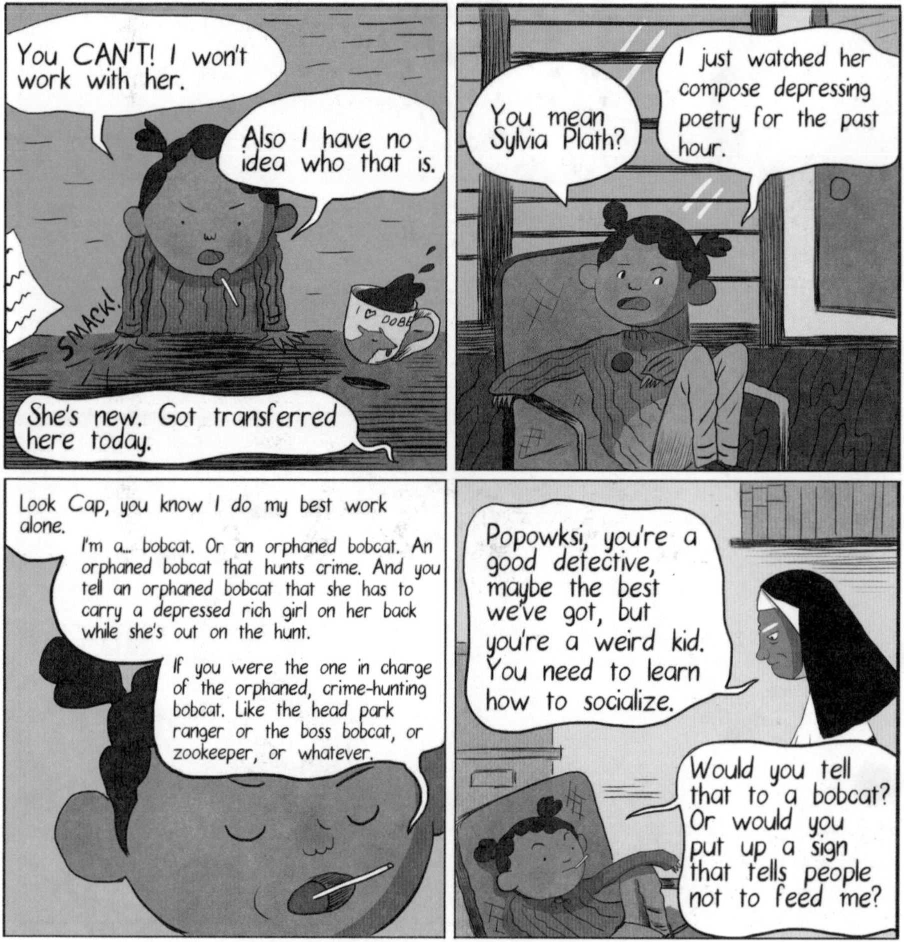
You CAN'T! I won't work with her.
Also I have no idea who that is.
SMACK!
I ♡ DOBE
She's new. Got transferred here today.
You mean Sylvia Plath?
I just watched her compose depressing poetry for the past hour.
Look Cap, you know I do my best work alone.
I'm a... bobcat. Or an orphaned bobcat. An orphaned bobcat that hunts crime. And you tell an orphaned bobcat that she has to carry a depressed rich girl on her back while she's out on the hunt.
If you were the one in charge of the orphaned, crime-hunting bobcat. Like the head park ranger or the boss bobcat, or zookeeper, or whatever.
Popowksi, you're a good detective, maybe the best we've got, but you're a weird kid. You need to learn how to socialize.
Would you tell that to a bobcat? Or would you put up a sign that tells people not to feed me?

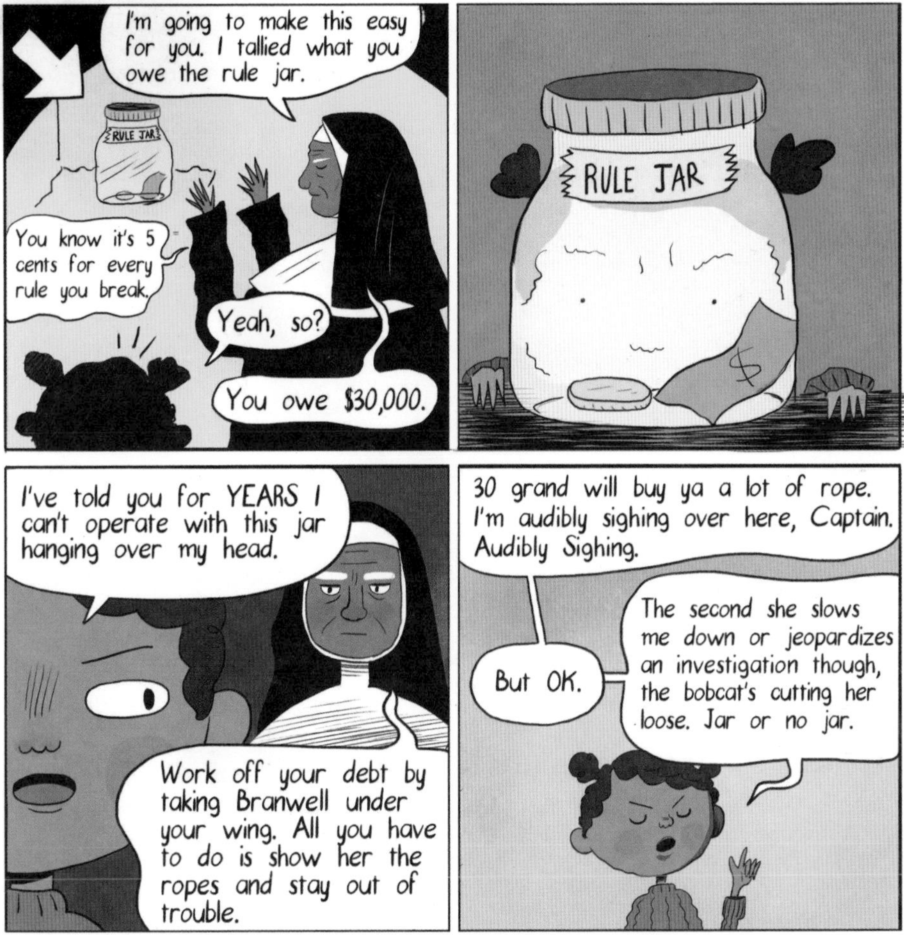
I'm going to make this easy for you. I tallied what you owe the rule jar.
RULE JAR
You know it's 5 cents for every rule you break.
Yeah, so?
You owe $30,000.
RULE JAR
I've told you for YEARS I can't operate with this jar hanging over my head.
Work off your debt by taking Branwell under your wing. All you have to do is show her the ropes and stay out of trouble.
30 grand will buy ya a lot of rope. I'm audibly sighing over here, Captain. Audibly Sighing.
But OK.
The second she slows me down or jeopardizes an investigation though, the bobcat's cutting her loose. Jar or no jar.

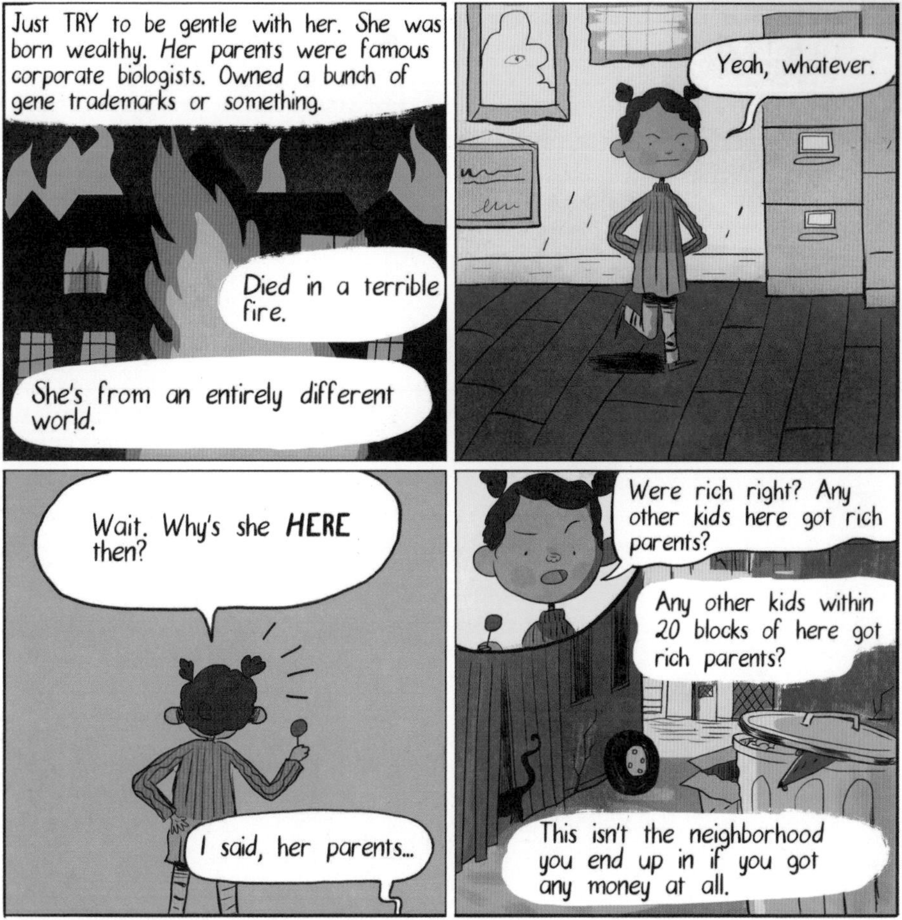

Just TRY to be gentle with her. She was born wealthy. Her parents were famous corporate biologists. Owned a bunch of gene trademarks or something.
Died in a terrible fire.
She's from an entirely different world.
Yeah, whatever.
Wait. Why's she HERE then?
I said, her parents...
Were rich right? Any other kids here got rich parents?
Any other kids within 20 blocks of here got rich parents?
This isn't the neighborhood you end up in if you got any money at all.

Only reason you put a billionaire k[id] here is to hide 'em. And why do you wanna hide 'em? She's irritating. Walking around reciting Smith's lyrics, clearly has no ... work ethic. I'd ... hide ... her. Put her in a ... lowe... ...ewhere. But maybe ... maybe ... you had to you also ... ... you murdered her family. accident. Hid... an heir. Where's ... Where's ... follow the money, we might find who burned

POPOWSKI!

POP....

Good meeting Cap. Gonna go bond with my new partner. Sure we're opposites, but often that's a formula for meaningful friendships!

The Branwells are a CLOSED CASE Popowski!!!!

This is when she busted that live wig gambling ring. This is when she caught the hoof hand killer.

Hook hand?

Hoof.

This is when she solved the case of the **cryborg**. Which is the kinda offensive name the newspaper gave that android thief that would weep during his crimes.

This is when she solved the **mer-murders**. Again the press ignores the fact that they weren't really merpeople, they were more like fish with human faces.

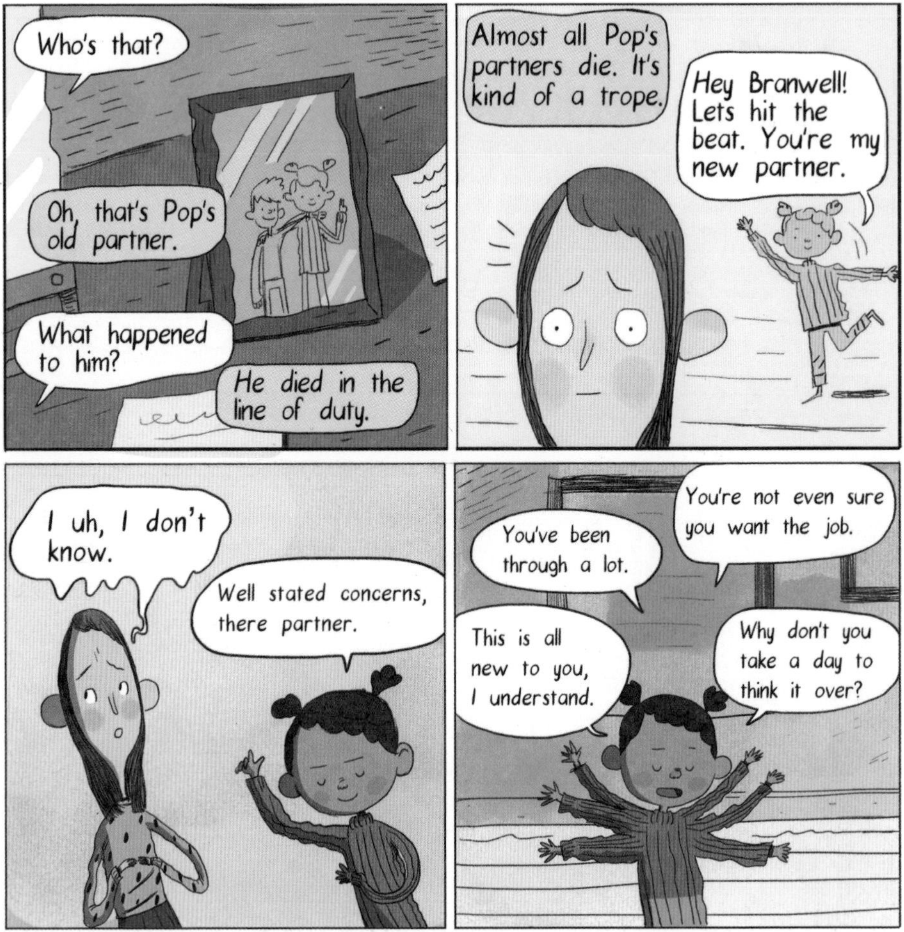
Who's that?
Oh, that's Pop's old partner.
What happened to him?
He died in the line of duty.
Almost all Pop's partners die. It's kind of a trope.
Hey Branwell! Lets hit the beat. You're my new partner.
I uh, I don't know.
Well stated concerns, there partner.
You've been through a lot.
You're not even sure you want the job.
This is all new to you, I understand.
Why don't you take a day to think it over?

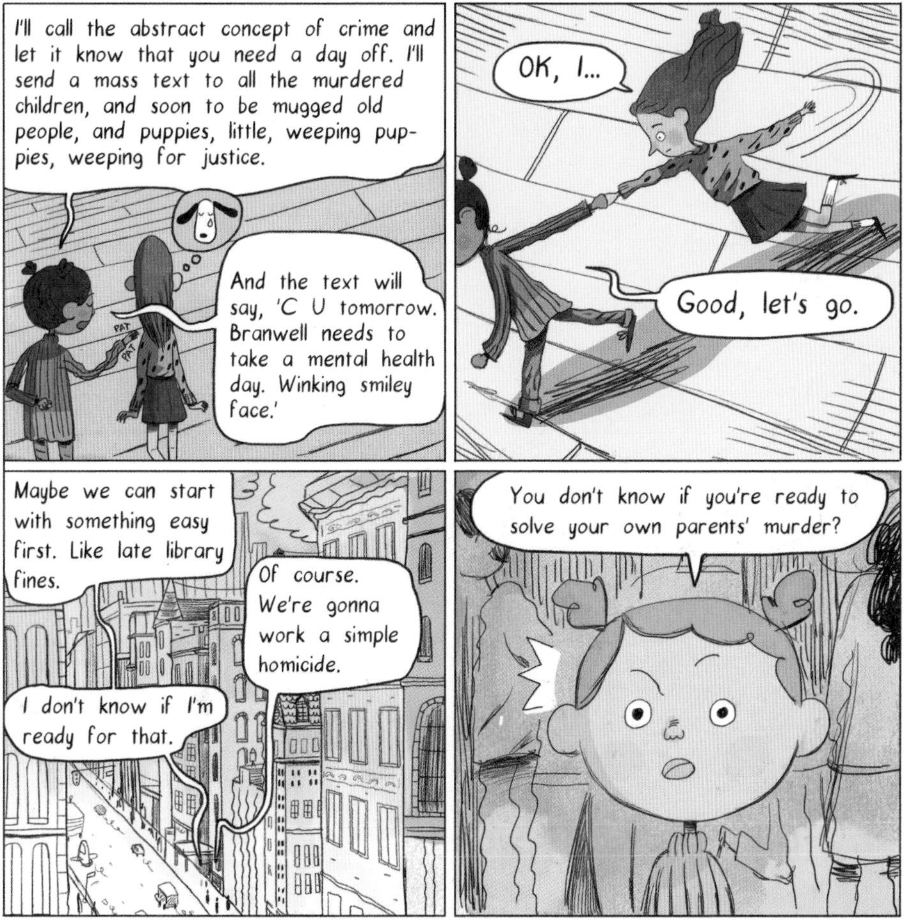
I'll call the abstract concept of crime and let it know that you need a day off. I'll send a mass text to all the murdered children, and soon to be mugged old people, and puppies, little, weeping pup-pies, weeping for justice.
PAT
PAT
And the text will say, 'C U tomorrow. Branwell needs to take a mental health day. Winking smiley face.'
OK, I...
Good, let's go.
Maybe we can start with something easy first. Like late library fines.
Of course. We're gonna work a simple homicide.
I don't know if I'm ready for that.
You don't know if you're ready to solve your own parents' murder?

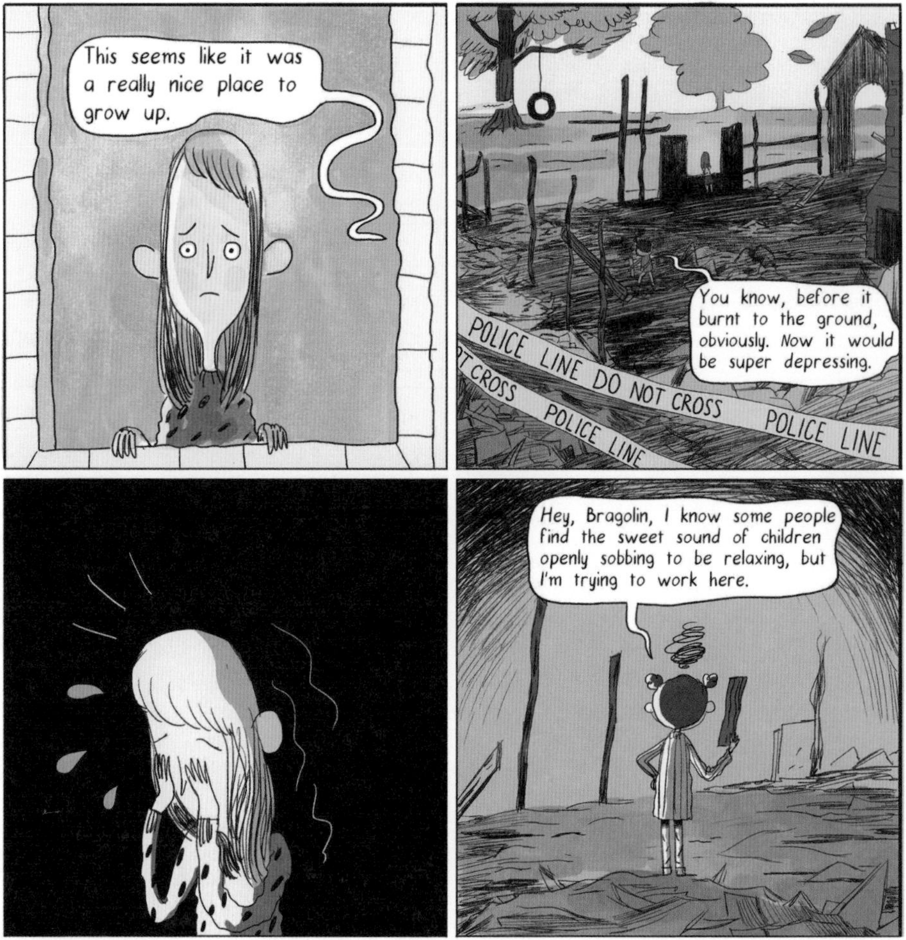
This seems like it was a really nice place to grow up.
You know, before it burnt to the ground, obviously. Now it would be super depressing.
POLICE LINE DO NOT CROSS POLICE LINE
POLICE LINE
Hey, Bragolin, I know some people find the sweet sound of children openly sobbing to be relaxing, but I'm trying to work here.

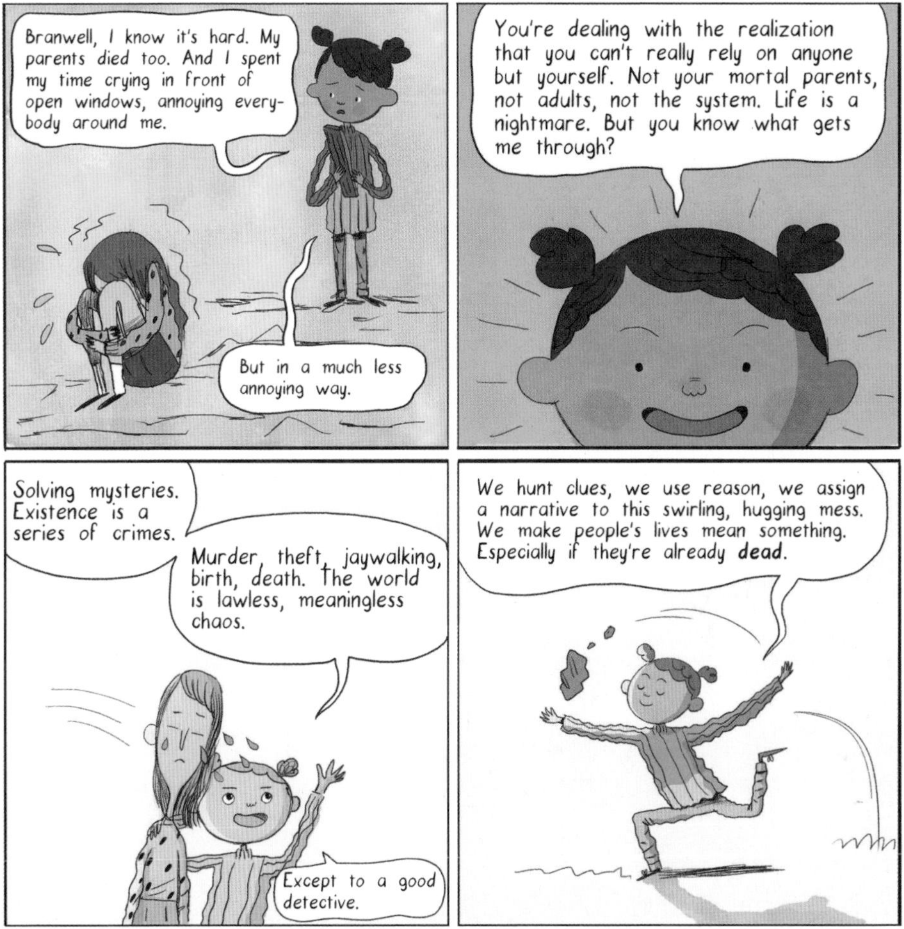
Branwell, I know it's hard. My parents died too. And I spent my time crying in front of open windows, annoying every-body around me.
But in a much less annoying way.
You're dealing with the realization that you can't really rely on anyone but yourself. Not your mortal parents, not adults, not the system. Life is a nightmare. But you know what gets me through?
Solving mysteries. Existence is a series of crimes.
Murder, theft, jaywalking, birth, death. The world is lawless, meaningless chaos.
Except to a good detective.
We hunt clues, we use reason, we assign a narrative to this swirling, hugging mess. We make people's lives mean something. Especially if they're already **dead**.

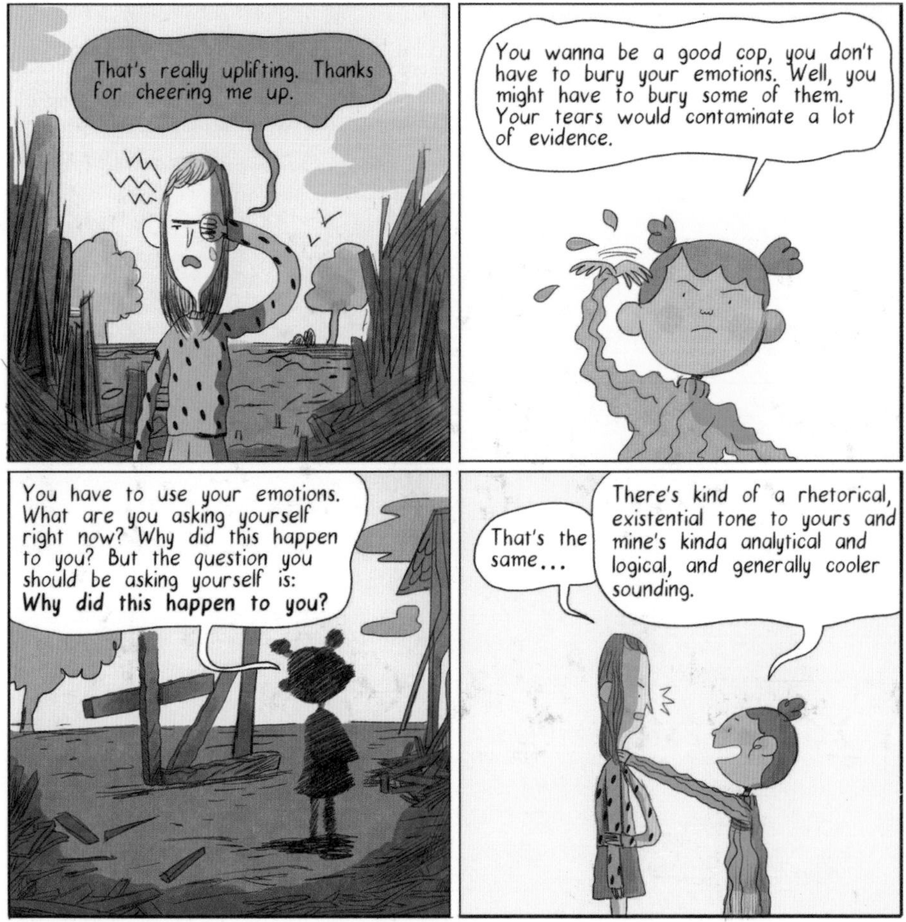
That's really uplifting. Thanks for cheering me up.
You wanna be a good cop, you don't have to bury your emotions. Well, you might have to bury some of them. Your tears would contaminate a lot of evidence.
You have to use your emotions. What are you asking yourself right now? Why did this happen to you? But the question you should be asking yourself is: **Why did this happen to you?**
That's the same...
There's kind of a rhetorical, existential tone to yours and mine's kinda analytical and logical, and generally cooler sounding.

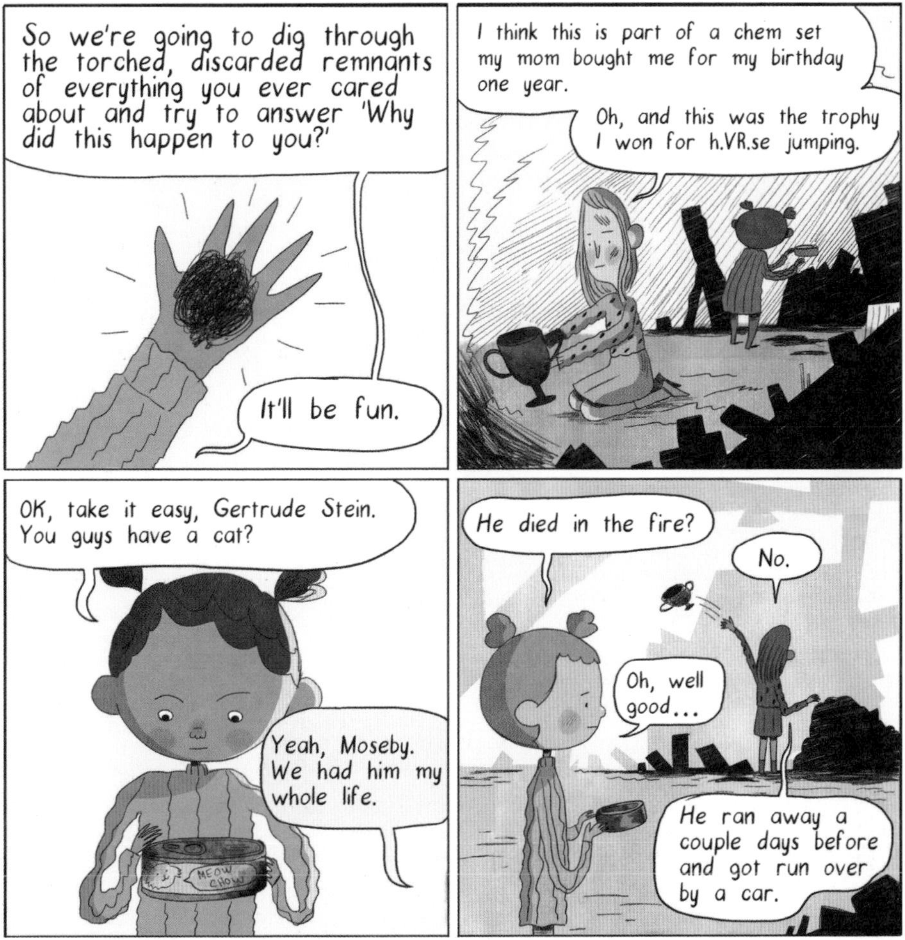
So we're going to dig through the torched, discarded remnants of everything you ever cared about and try to answer 'Why did this happen to you?'
It'll be fun.
I think this is part of a chem set my mom bought me for my birthday one year.
Oh, and this was the trophy I won for h.VR.se jumping.
OK, take it easy, Gertrude Stein. You guys have a cat?
Yeah, Moseby. We had him my whole life.
MEOW CHOW
He died in the fire?
No.
Oh, well good...
He ran away a couple days before and got run over by a car.

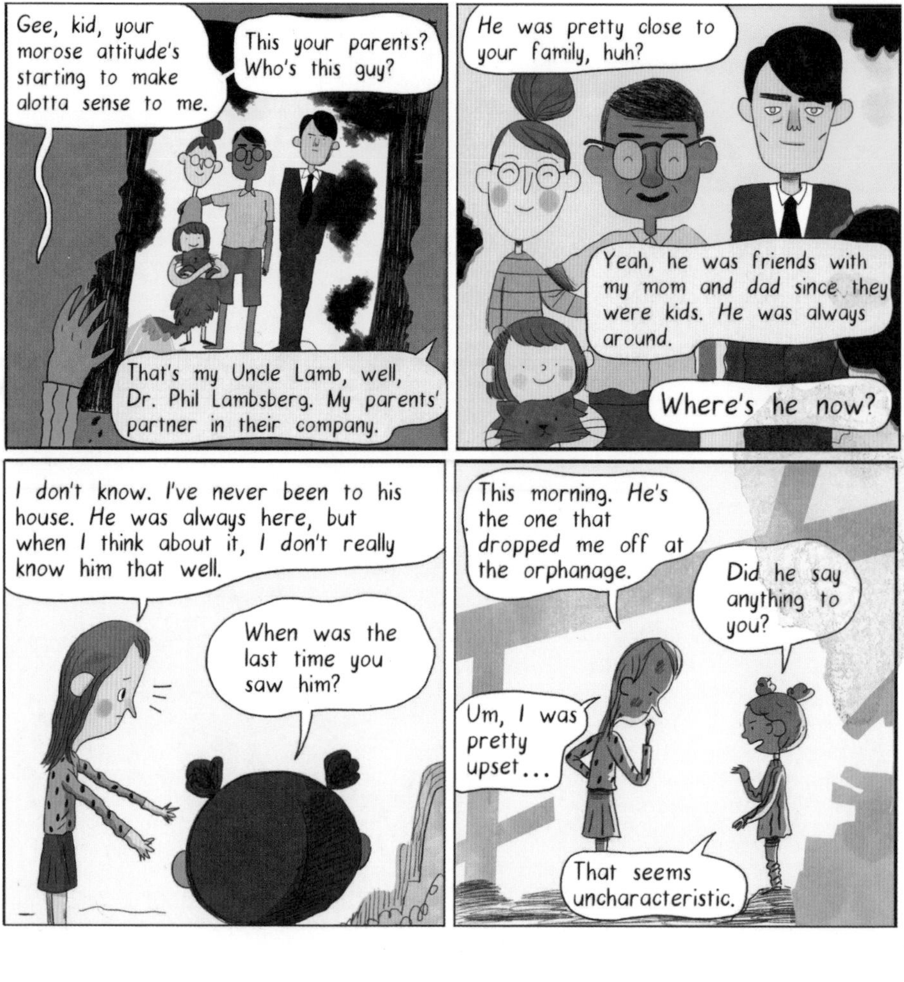
Gee, kid, your morose attitude's starting to make alotta sense to me.
This your parents? Who's this guy?
That's my Uncle Lamb, well, Dr. Phil Lambsberg. My parents' partner in their company.
He was pretty close to your family, huh?
Yeah, he was friends with my mom and dad since they were kids. He was always around.
Where's he now?
I don't know. I've never been to his house. He was always here, but when I think about it, I don't really know him that well.
When was the last time you saw him?
This morning. He's the one that dropped me off at the orphanage.
Did he say anything to you?
Um, I was pretty upset...
That seems uncharacteristic.

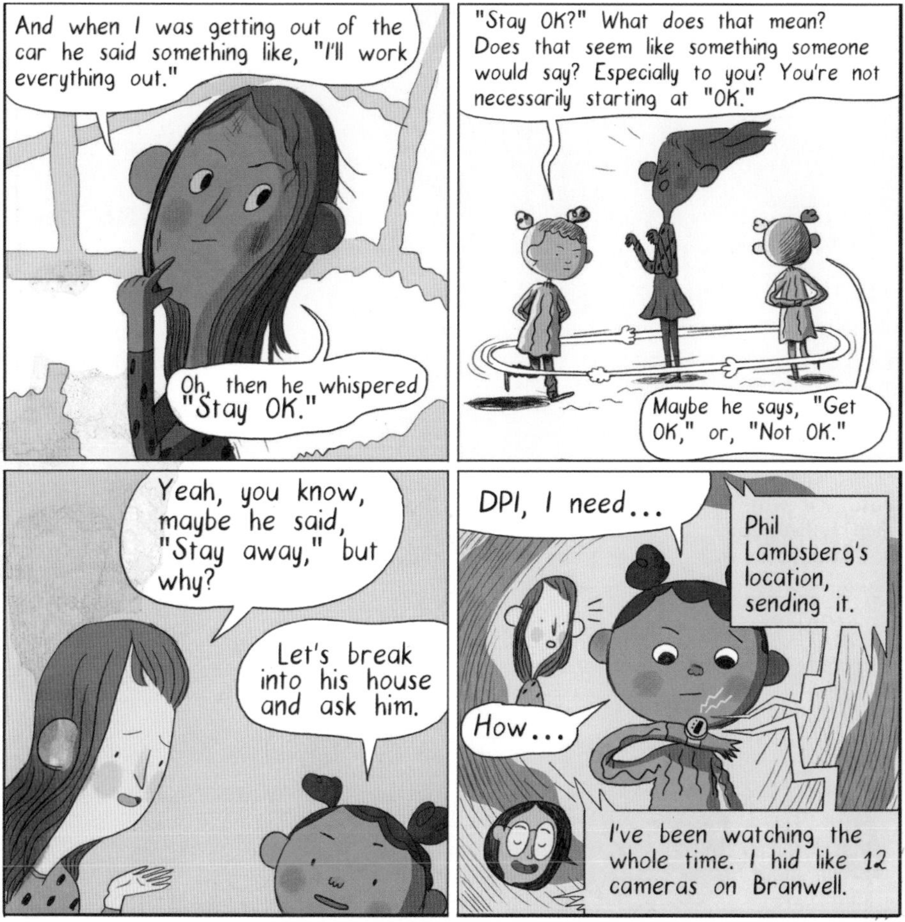

And when I was getting out of the car he said something like, "I'll work everything out."
Oh, then he whispered "Stay OK."
"Stay OK?" What does that mean? Does that seem like something someone would say? Especially to you? You're not necessarily starting at "OK."
Maybe he says, "Get OK," or, "Not OK."
Yeah, you know, maybe he said, "Stay away," but why?
Let's break into his house and ask him.
DPI, I need...
Phil Lambsberg's location, sending it.
How...
I've been watching the whole time. I hid like 12 cameras on Branwell.

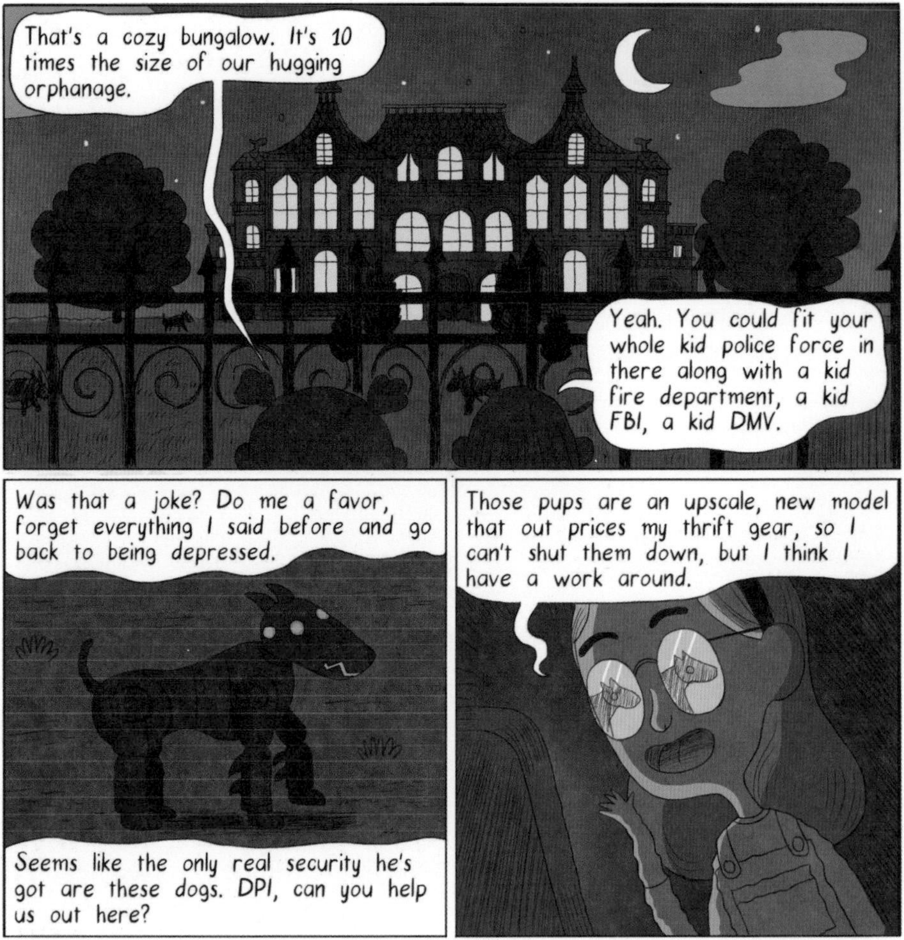
That's a cozy bungalow. It's 10 times the size of our hugging orphanage.
Yeah. You could fit your whole kid police force in there along with a kid fire department, a kid FBI, a kid DMV.
Was that a joke? Do me a favor, forget everything I said before and go back to being depressed.
Seems like the only real security he's got are these dogs. DPI, can you help us out here?
Those pups are an upscale, new model that out prices my thrift gear, so I can't shut them down, but I think I have a work around.

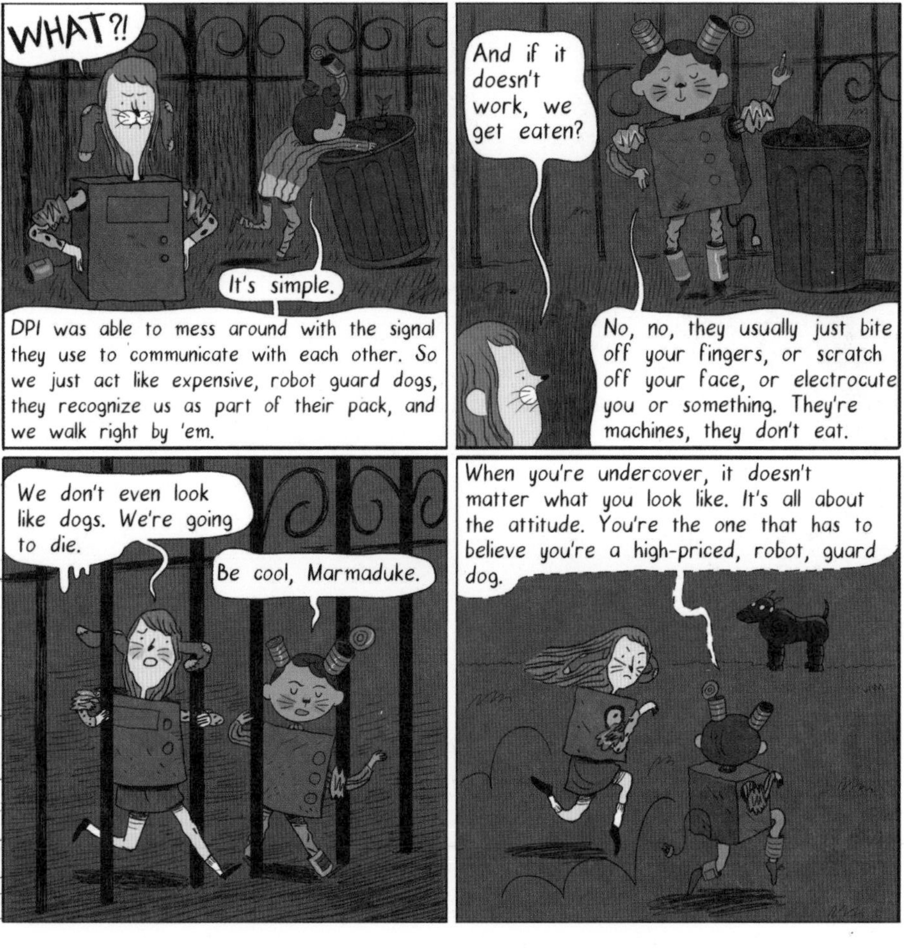
WHAT?!
It's simple.
DPI was able to mess around with the signal they use to communicate with each other. So we just act like expensive, robot guard dogs, they recognize us as part of their pack, and we walk right by 'em.
And if it doesn't work, we get eaten?
No, no, they usually just bite off your fingers, or scratch off your face, or electrocute you or something. They're machines, they don't eat.
We don't even look like dogs. We're going to die.
Be cool, Marmaduke.
When you're undercover, it doesn't matter what you look like. It's all about the attitude. You're the one that has to believe you're a high-priced, robot, guard dog.

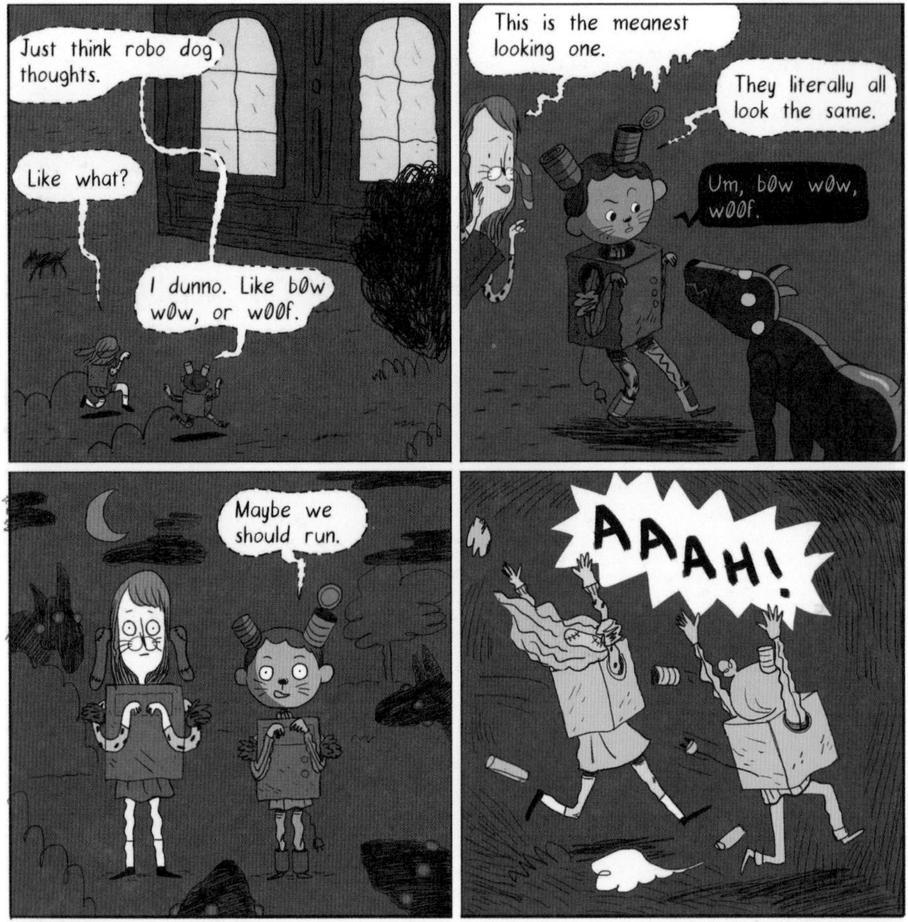
Just think robo dog thoughts.
Like what?
I dunno. Like bØw wØw, or wØØf.
This is the meanest looking one.
They literally all look the same.
Um, bØw wØw, wØØf.
Maybe we should run.
AAAH!

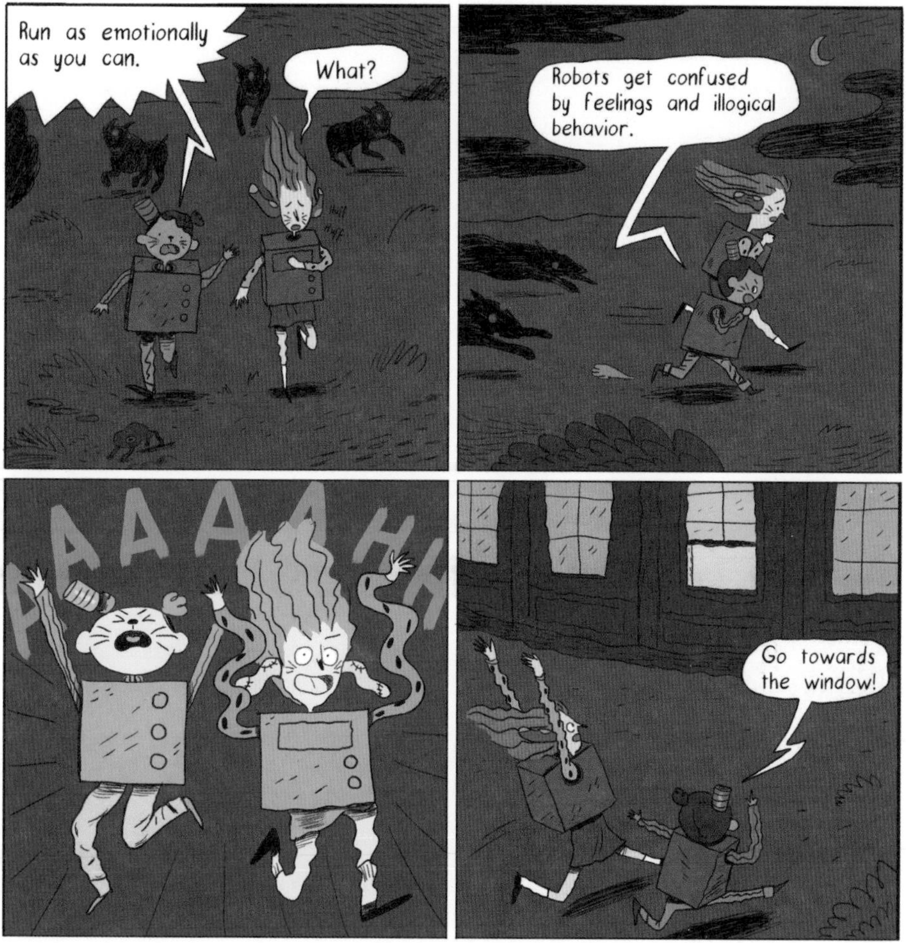
Run as emotionally as you can.
What?
Huff Huff
Robots get confused by feelings and illogical behavior.
AAAAAHH
Go towards the window!

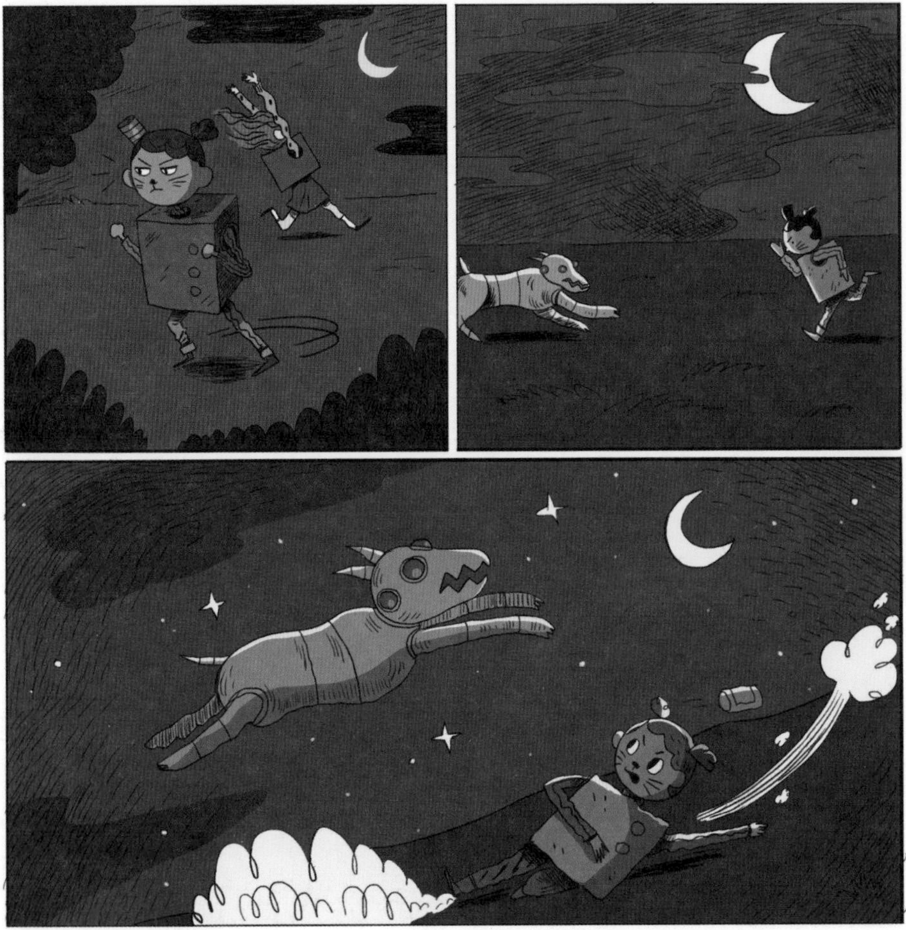

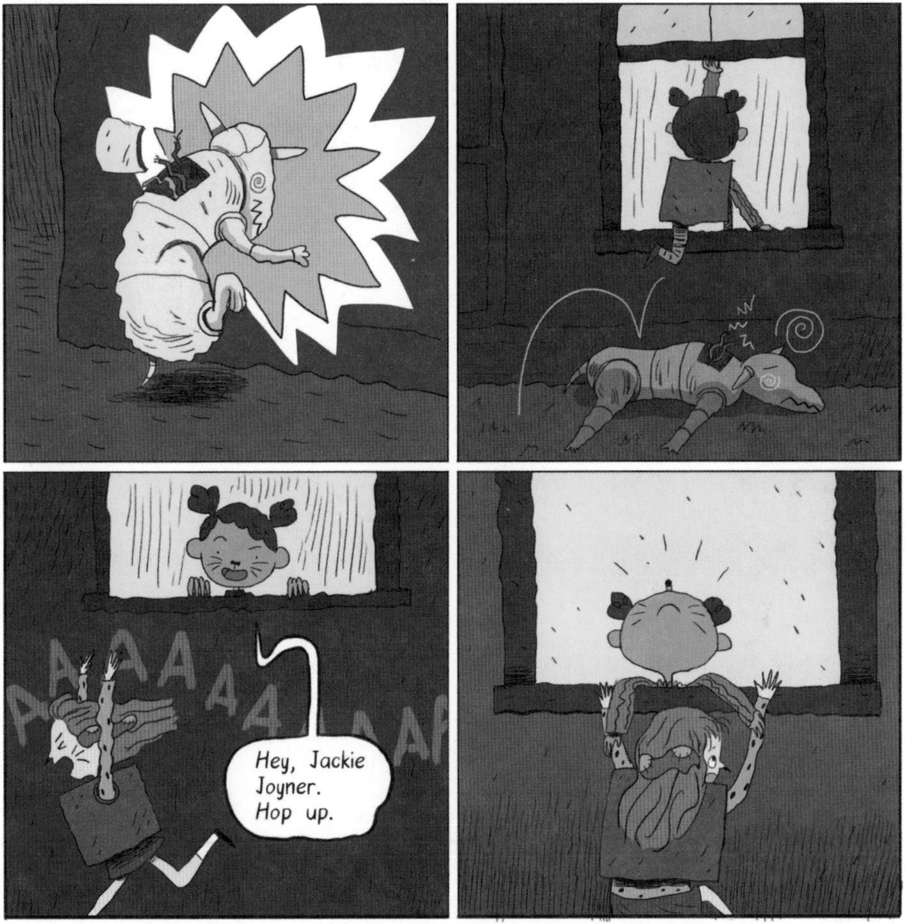
Hey, Jackie Joyner. Hop up.

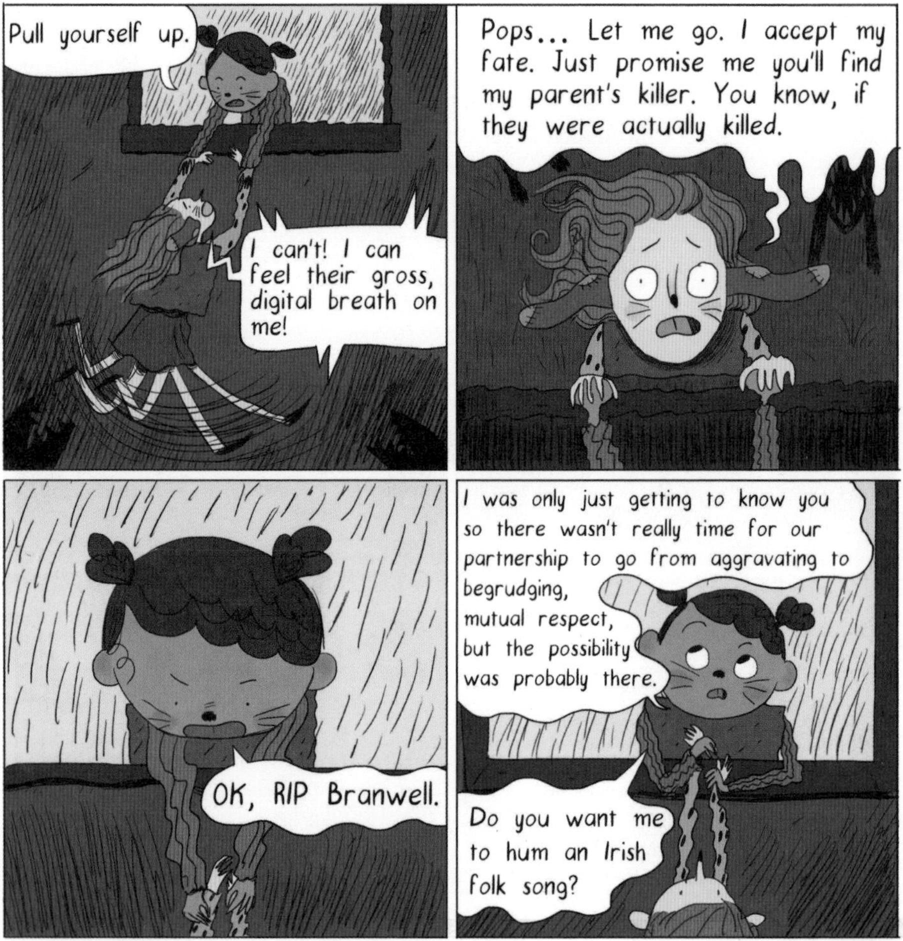

Pull yourself up.
I can't! I can feel their gross, digital breath on me!
Pops... Let me go. I accept my fate. Just promise me you'll find my parent's killer. You know, if they were actually killed.
OK, RIP Branwell.
I was only just getting to know you so there wasn't really time for our partnership to go from aggravating to begrudging, mutual respect, but the possibility was probably there.
Do you want me to hum an Irish folk song?

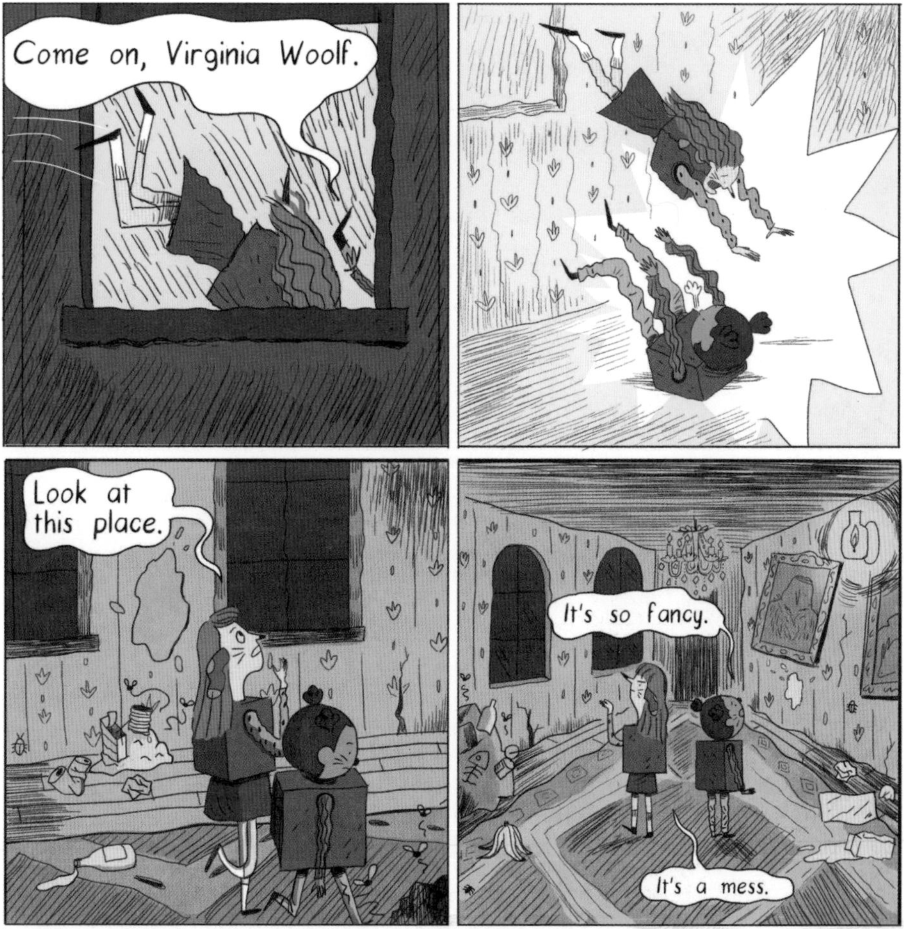
Come on, Virginia Woolf.
Look at this place.
It's so fancy.
It's a mess.

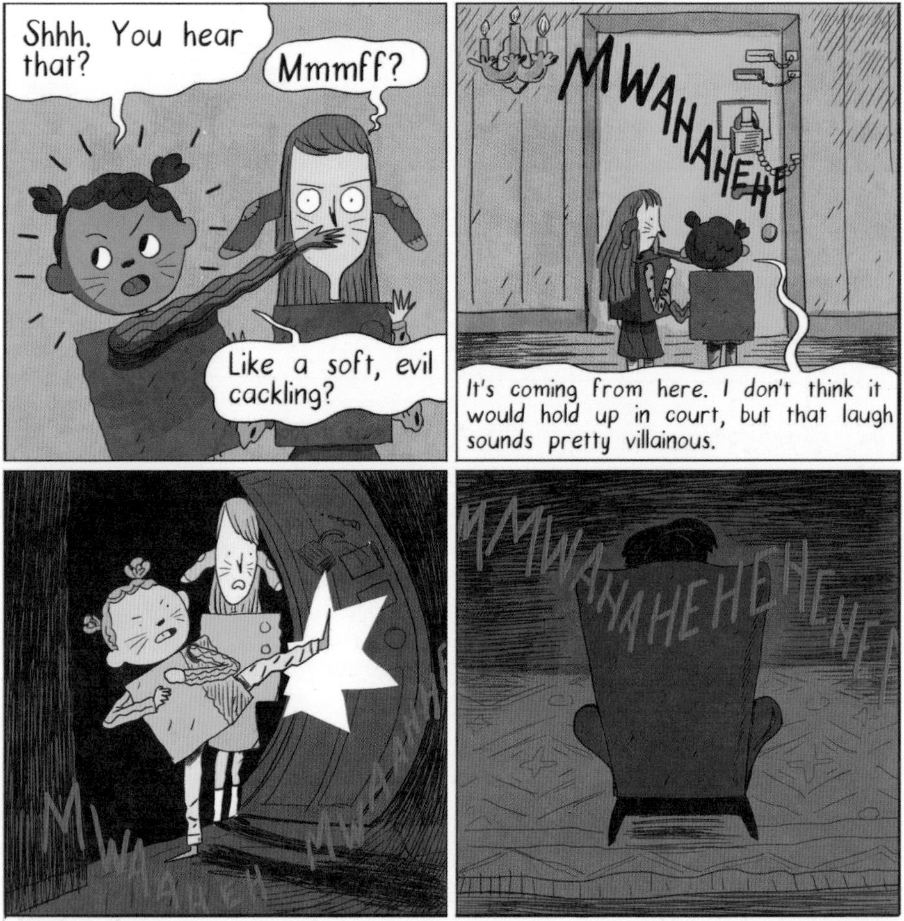
Shhh. You hear that?
Mmmff?
Like a soft, evil cackling?
MWAHAHEHE
It's coming from here. I don't think it would hold up in court, but that laugh sounds pretty villainous.

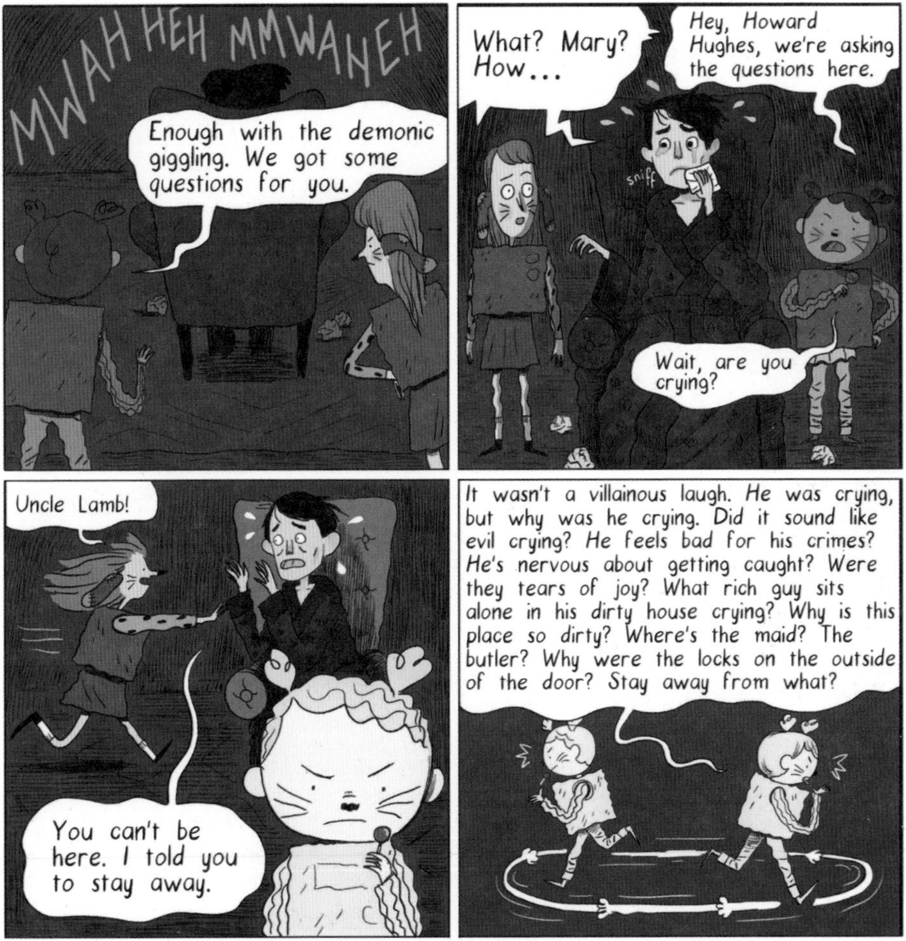
MWAH HEH MMWAHEH
Enough with the demonic giggling. We got some questions for you.
What? Mary? How...
Hey, Howard Hughes, we're asking the questions here.
sniff
Wait, are you crying?
Uncle Lamb!
You can't be here. I told you to stay away.
It wasn't a villainous laugh. He was crying, but why was he crying. Did it sound like evil crying? He feels bad for his crimes? He's nervous about getting caught? Were they tears of joy? What rich guy sits alone in his dirty house crying? Why is this place so dirty? Where's the maid? The butler? Why were the locks on the outside of the door? Stay away from what?

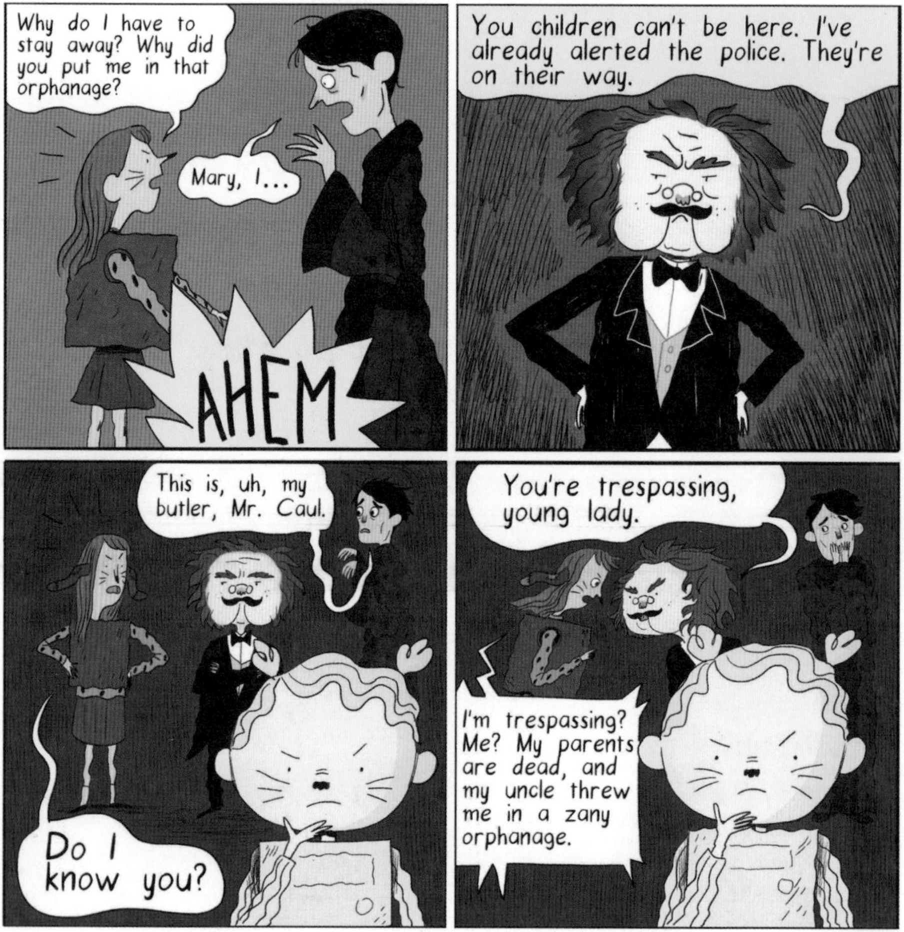
Why do I have to stay away? Why did you put me in that orphanage?
Mary, I...
AHEM
You children can't be here. I've already alerted the police. They're on their way.
This is, uh, my butler, Mr. Caul.
Do I know you?
You're trespassing, young lady.
I'm trespassing? Me? My parents are dead, and my uncle threw me in a zany orphanage.

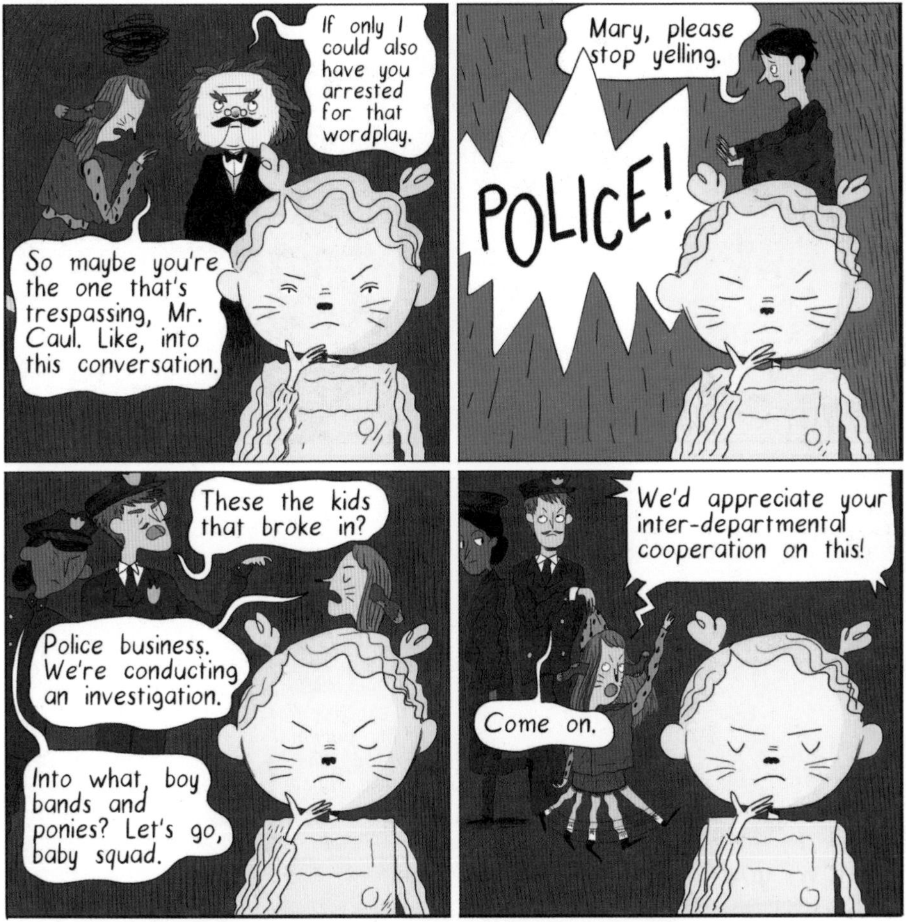
If only I could also have you arrested for that wordplay.
So maybe you're the one that's trespassing, Mr. Caul. Like, into this conversation.
Mary, please stop yelling.
POLICE!
These the kids that broke in?
Police business. We're conducting an investigation.
Into what, boy bands and ponies? Let's go, baby squad.
We'd appreciate your inter-departmental cooperation on this!
Come on.

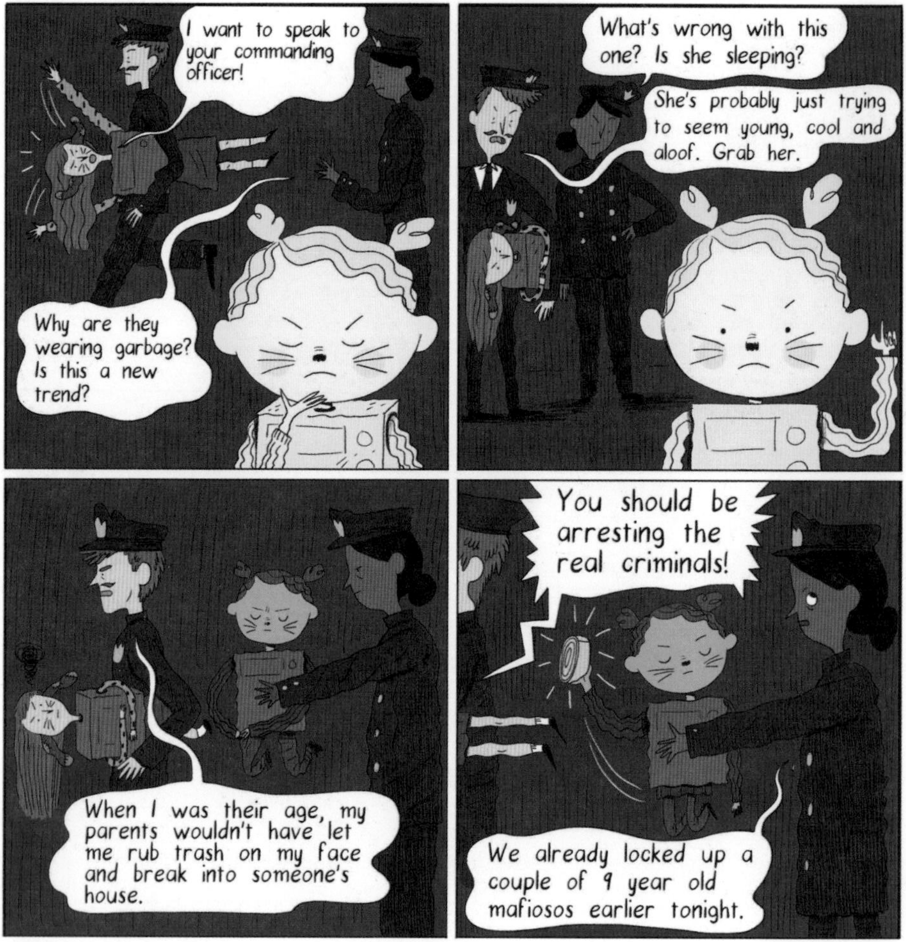
I want to speak to your commanding officer!
Why are they wearing garbage? Is this a new trend?
What's wrong with this one? Is she sleeping?
She's probably just trying to seem young, cool and aloof. Grab her.
When I was their age, my parents wouldn't have let me rub trash on my face and break into someone's house.
You should be arresting the real criminals!
We already locked up a couple of 9 year old mafiosos earlier tonight.

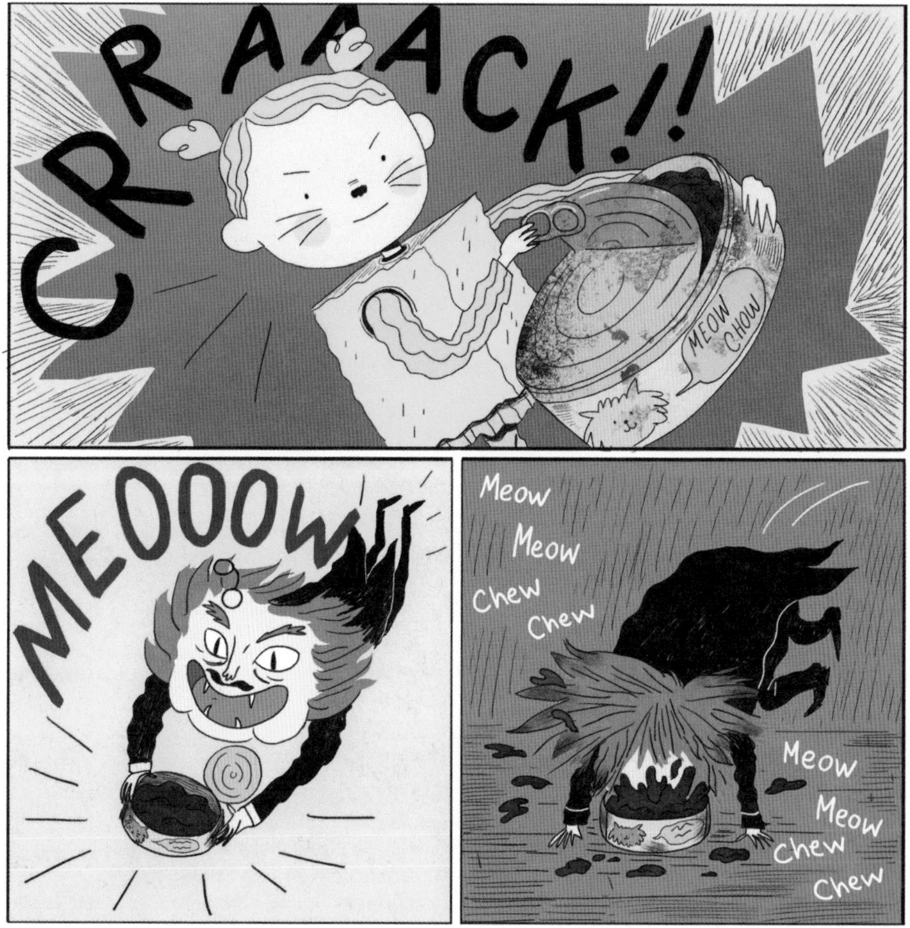
CRAAACK!!
MEOW CHOW
MEOOOW!!
Meow
Meow
Chew
Chew
Meow
Meow
Chew
Chew

What?

Time to spill the beans, Mr. Caul aka Moseby, the Branwell family cat.

What? I'm the butler. You're being purrfectly ridiculous. I'm humeown.

Ahem. Human.

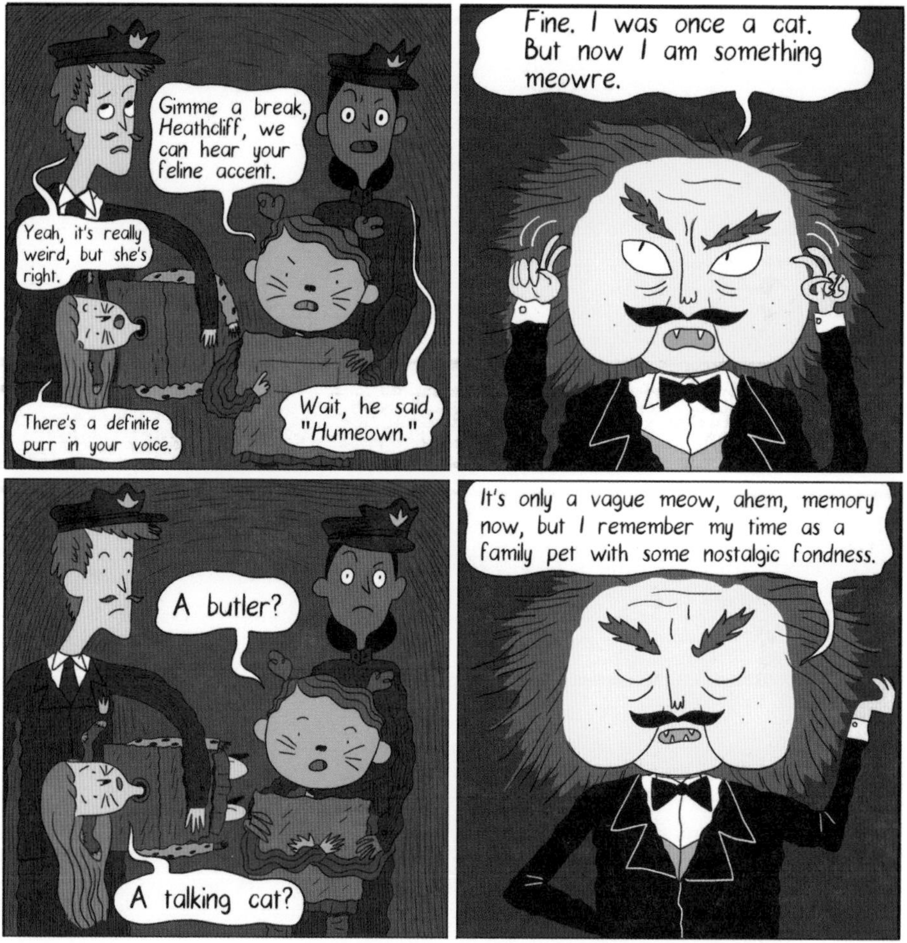
Gimme a break, Heathcliff, we can hear your feline accent.
Yeah, it's really weird, but she's right.
There's a definite purr in your voice.
Wait, he said, "Humeown."
Fine. I was once a cat. But now I am something meowre.
A butler?
A talking cat?
It's only a vague meow, ahem, memory now, but I remember my time as a family pet with some nostalgic fondness.

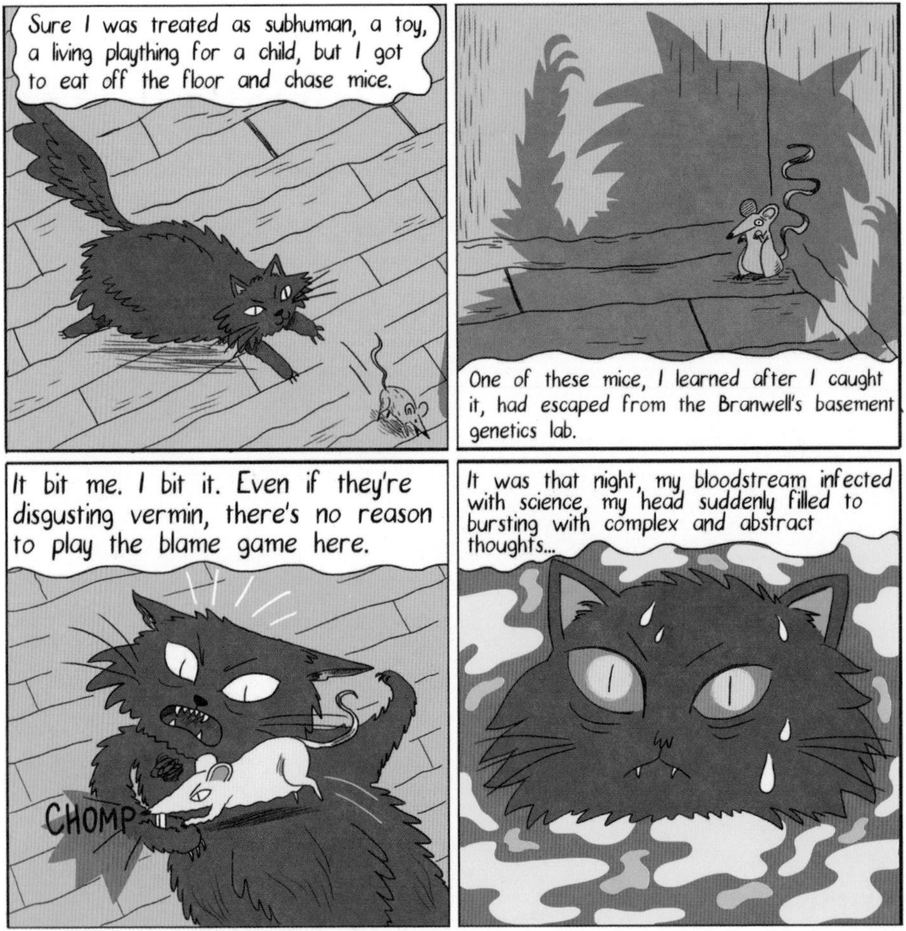
Sure I was treated as subhuman, a toy, a living plaything for a child, but I got to eat off the floor and chase mice.
One of these mice, I learned after I caught it, had escaped from the Branwell's basement genetics lab.
It bit me. I bit it. Even if they're disgusting vermin, there's no reason to play the blame game here.
CHOMP
It was that night, my bloodstream infected with science, my head suddenly filled to bursting with complex and abstract thoughts...

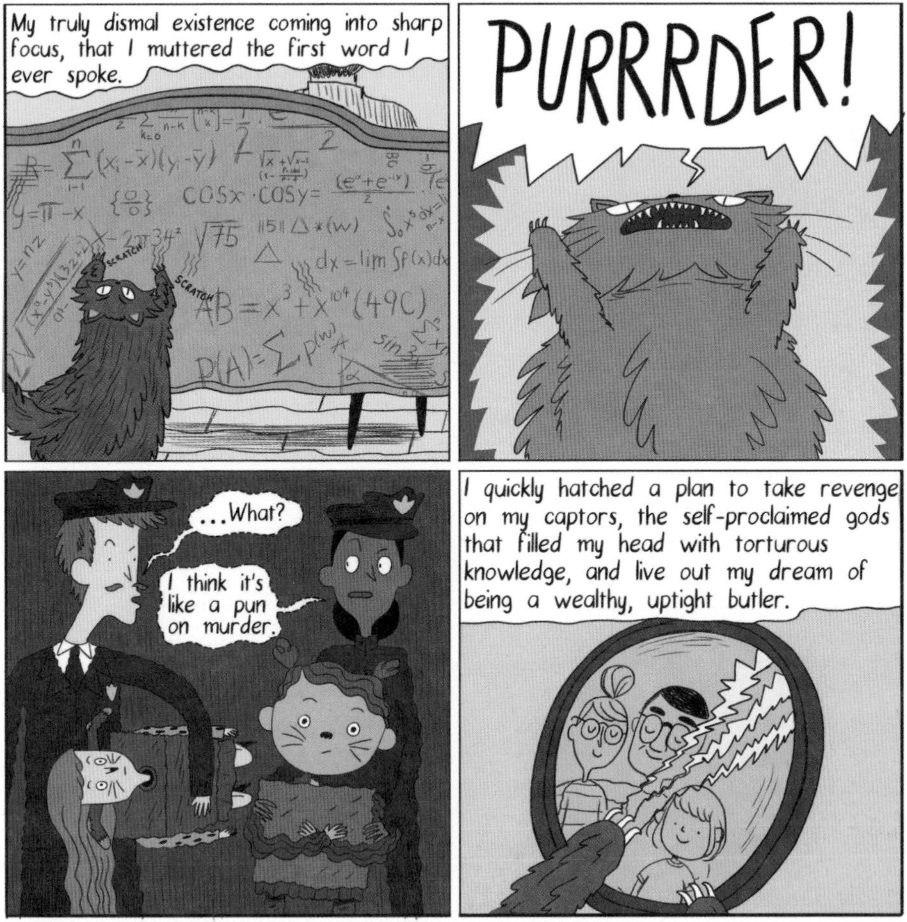
My truly dismal existence coming into sharp focus, that I muttered the first word I ever spoke.
SCRATCH
SCRATCH
PURRRDER!
...What?
I think it's like a pun on murder.
I quickly hatched a plan to take revenge on my captors, the self-proclaimed gods that filled my head with torturous knowledge, and live out my dream of being a wealthy, uptight butler.

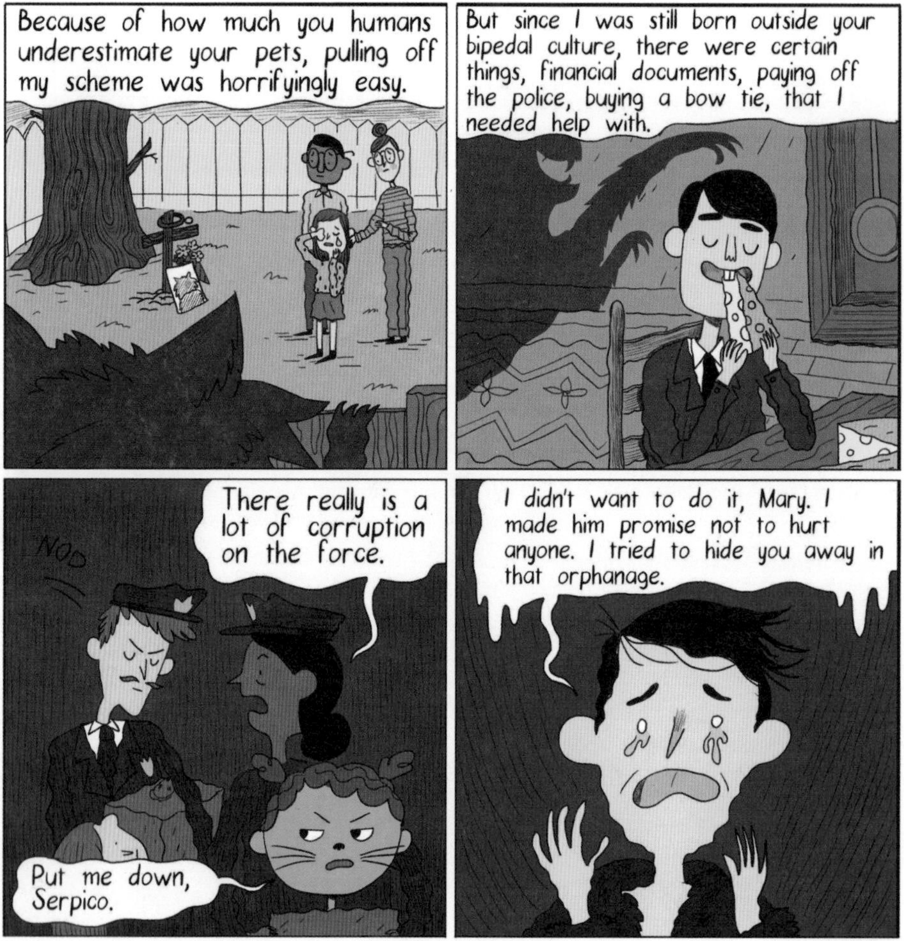
Because of how much you humans underestimate your pets, pulling off my scheme was horrifyingly easy.
But since I was still born outside your bipedal culture, there were certain things, financial documents, paying off the police, buying a bow tie, that I needed help with.
NOD
There really is a lot of corruption on the force.
Put me down, Serpico.
I didn't want to do it, Mary. I made him promise not to hurt anyone. I tried to hide you away in that orphanage.

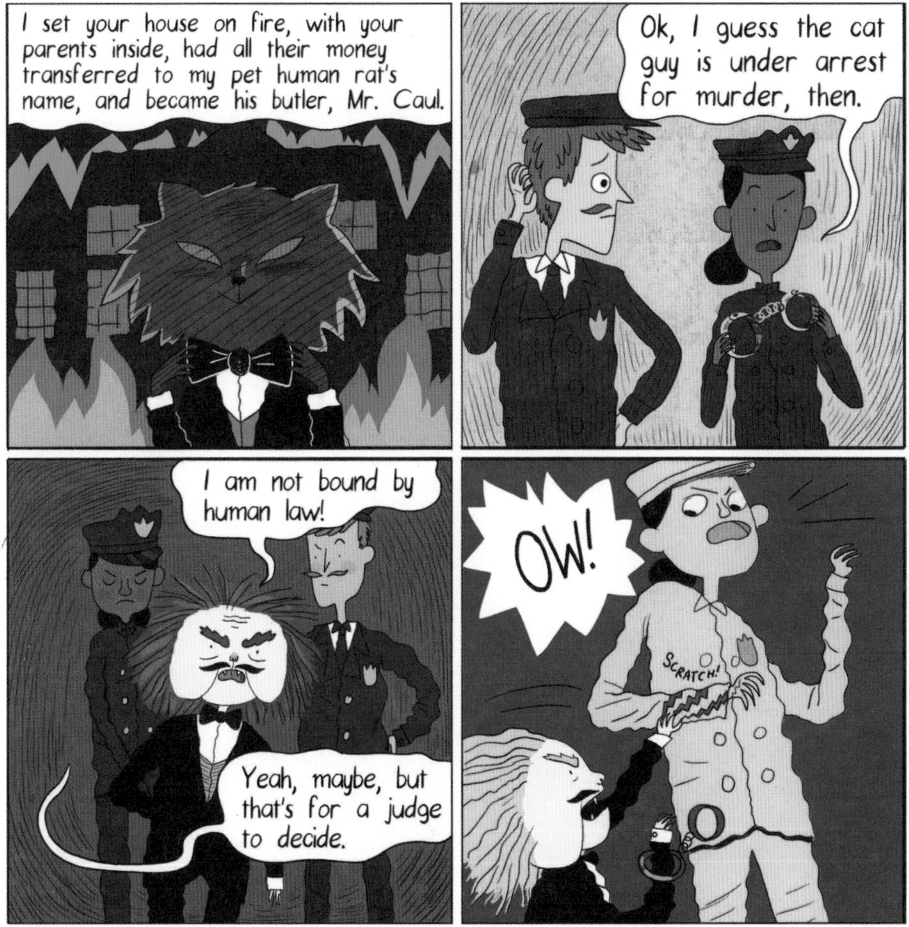
I set your house on fire, with your parents inside, had all their money transferred to my pet human rat's name, and became his butler, Mr. Caul.
Ok, I guess the cat guy is under arrest for murder, then.
I am not bound by human law!
Yeah, maybe, but that's for a judge to decide.
OW!
SCRATCH!

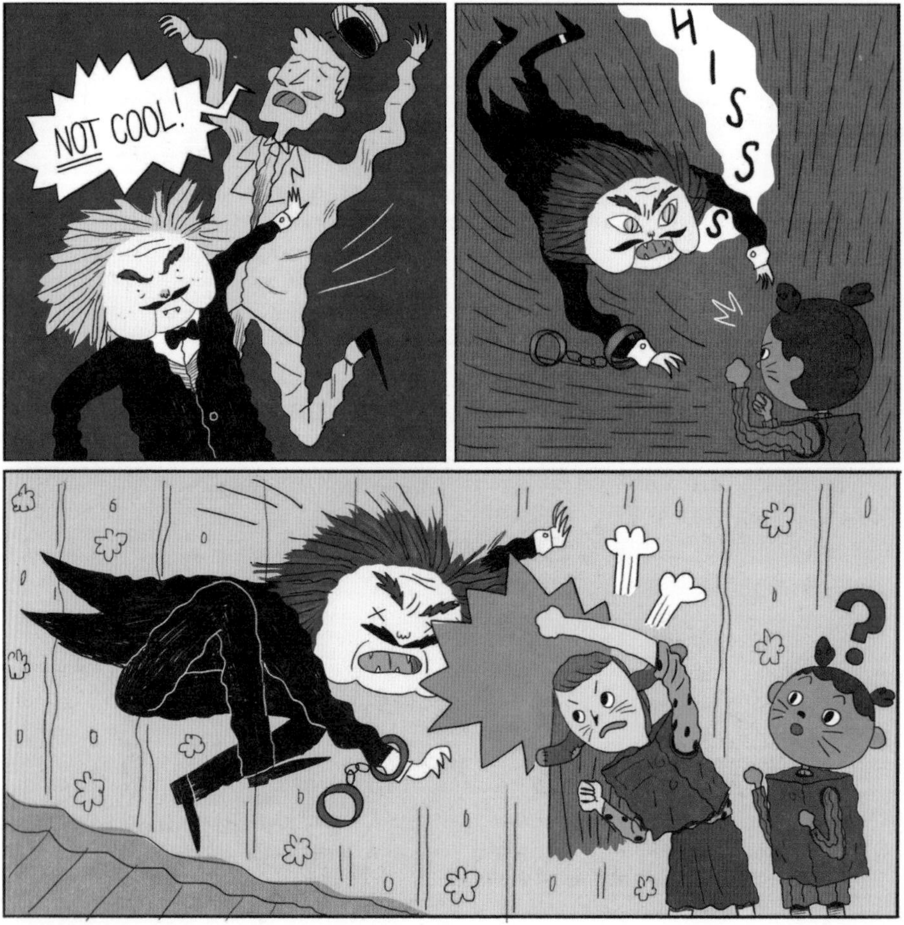
NOT COOL!
HISSS

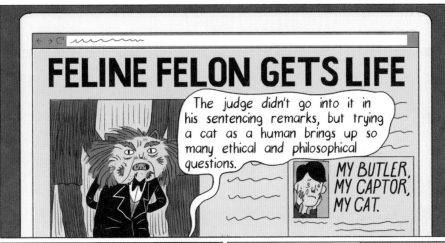

FELINE FELON GETS LIFE

The judge didn't go into it in his sentencing remarks, but trying a cat as a human brings up so many ethical and philosophical questions.

MY BUTLER, MY CAPTOR, MY CAT.

Is it his mutated DNA that makes him human or is it his capacity for evil?

Has society decided that our ability to commit crime is the defining characteristic of human culture?

Take it easy, Truman Capote.

You and Branwell made a great team. And you didn't even get her killed.

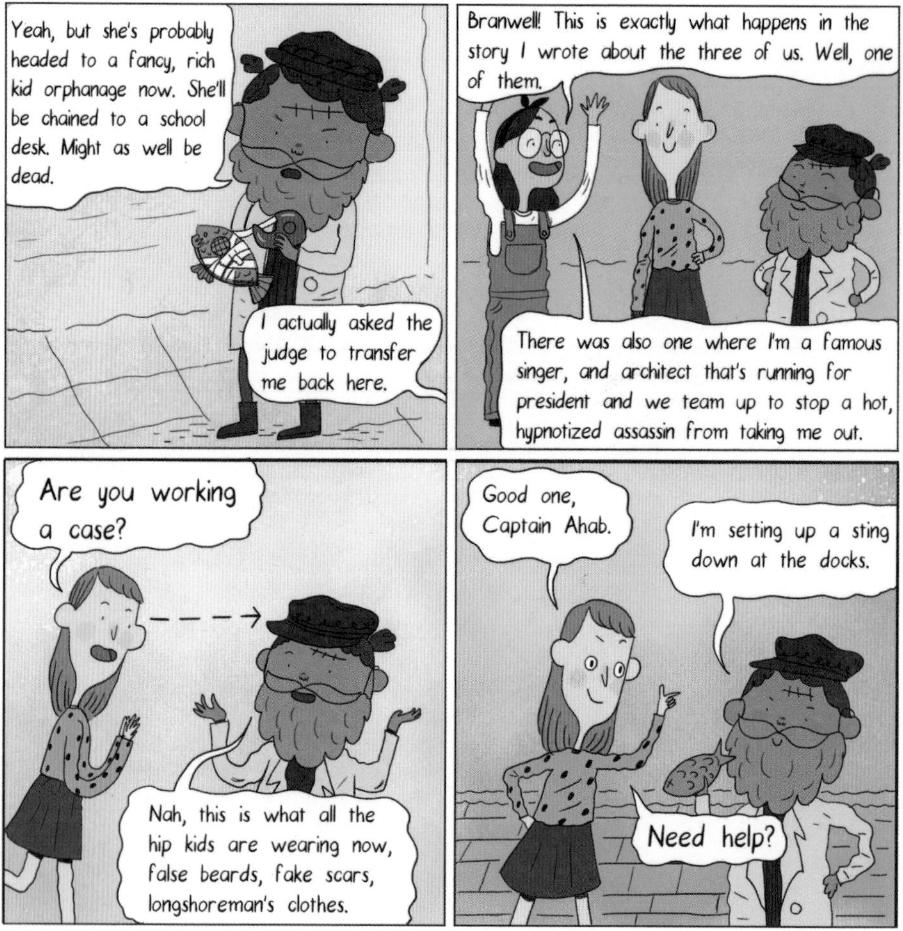
Yeah, but she's probably headed to a fancy, rich kid orphanage now. She'll be chained to a school desk. Might as well be dead.
I actually asked the judge to transfer me back here.
Branwell! This is exactly what happens in the story I wrote about the three of us. Well, one of them.
There was also one where I'm a famous singer, and architect that's running for president and we team up to stop a hot, hypnotized assassin from taking me out.
Are you working a case?
Nah, this is what all the hip kids are wearing now, false beards, fake scars, longshoreman's clothes.
Good one, Captain Ahab.
I'm setting up a sting down at the docks.
Need help?

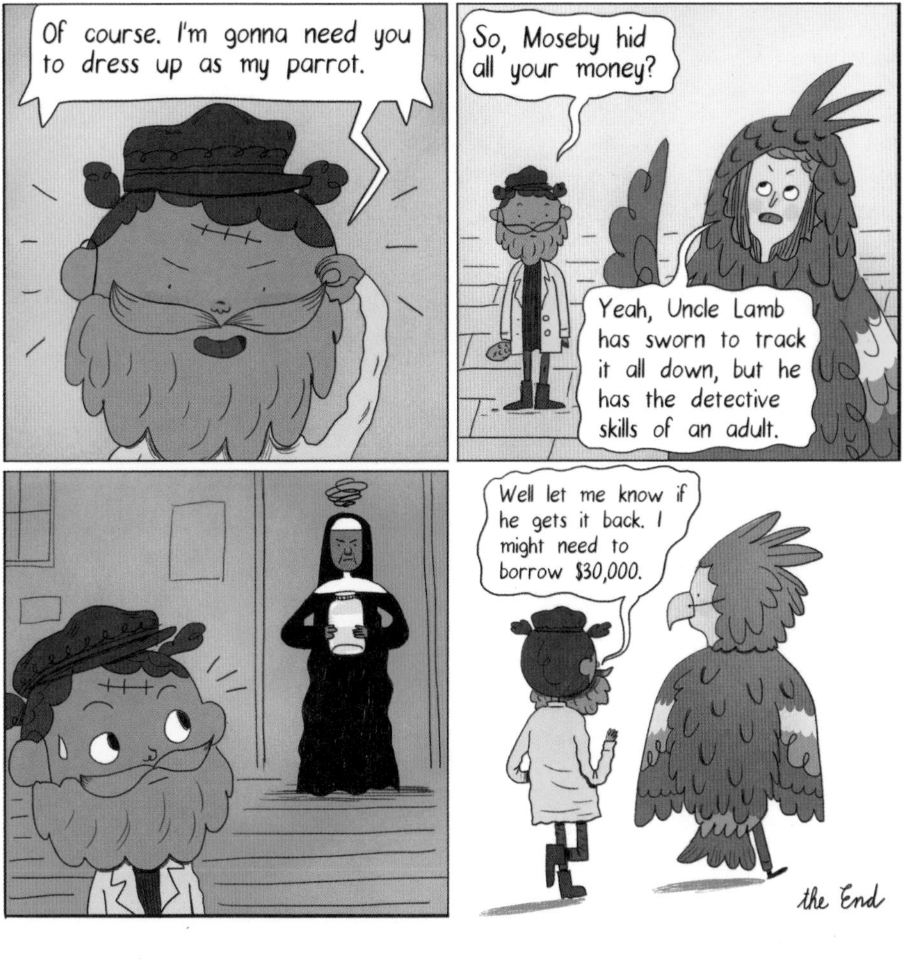
Of course. I'm gonna need you to dress up as my parrot.
So, Moseby hid all your money?
Yeah, Uncle Lamb has sworn to track it all down, but he has the detective skills of an adult.
Well let me know if he gets it back. I might need to borrow $30,000.
the End

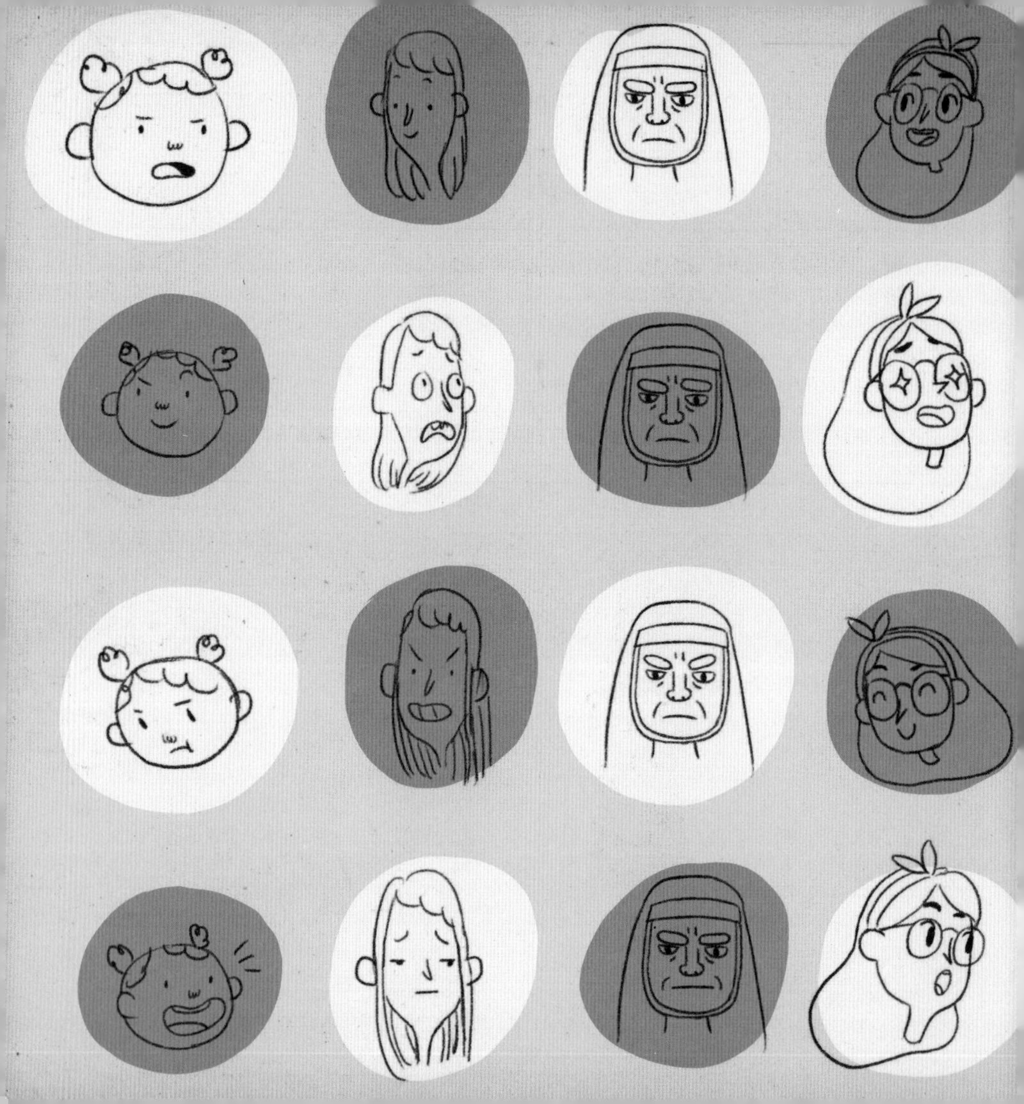